What would you do if a stranger gave you
something that turned out to be yours?

Also by Jenny Valentine

Finding Violet Park

Jenny Valentine

BROKEN SOUP

HarperCollins *Children's Books*

First published in Great Britain by HarperCollins *Children's Books* 2008
HarperCollins *Children's Books* is a division of HarperCollins *Publishers* Ltd
77-85 Fulham Palace Road, Hammersmith, London, W6 8JB

www.harpercollinschildrensbooks.co.uk

4

Copyright © Jenny Valentine 2008

ISBN 13: 978 0 00 722965 9
ISBN 10: 0 00 722965 8

Jenny Valentine asserts the moral right to be
identified as the author of the work.

Printed and bound in Great Britain by
Clays Ltd, St Ives plc

Mixed Sources
Product group from well-managed
forests and other controlled sources
www.fsc.org Cert no. SW-COC-1806
© 1996 Forest Stewardship Council

FSC is a non-profit international organisation established to promote the
responsible management of the world's forests. Products carrying the FSC
label are independently certified to assure consumers that they come
from forests that are managed to meet the social, economic and
ecological needs of present and future generations.

Find out more about HarperCollins and the environment at
www.harpercollins.co.uk/green

For
Molly and Ella,
Jess and Emma,
and Kate.
All great sisters.

one

It wasn't mine.

I didn't drop it, but the boy in the queue said I did.

It was a negative of a photograph, one on its own, all scratched and beaten up. I couldn't even see what it was a negative of because his finger and thumb were blotting out most of it. He was holding it out to me like nothing else was going to happen until I took it, like he had nothing else to do but wait.

I didn't want to take it. I said that. I said I didn't own a camera even, but the boy just stood there with this I-know-I'm-right look on his face.

He had a good face. Friendly eyes, wide mouth, all that. One of his top teeth was chipped; there was a bit missing. Still, a good face doesn't equal a good person. If you catch yourself thinking that, you need to stop.

All my friends were cracking up behind me. The girl at the counter was trying to give me my change and everybody in the queue was just staring. I couldn't think why he was doing this to me. I wondered if embarrassing strangers was one of the ways he got through his day. Maybe he walked around with a pile of random stuff in his pockets – not just negatives, but thimbles and condoms and glasses and handcuffs. I might be getting off lightly.

I didn't know what else to do, so I said thank you, who knows for what, and I went red like always, and I pulled a face at my friends like I was in on the joke. Then I shoved the negative in my bag with the oranges and milk and eggs, and he smiled.

All the way home I got, "What is it, Rowan?" and "Let's see" and "Nice smile" – a flock of seagulls in school uniform, shrieking and pointing and jumping around me. And I did my usual thing of taking something that's just happened apart in my head, until it's in little pieces all over the place and I can't fit it back together again. I wanted to know why he'd picked me out of everyone in the shop, and whether I should be glad about that or not. I thought about what he said (*you dropped this … no really … I'm sure*) and what I did (act like a rabbit in headlights, argue, give in). I was laughing about it on the outside, feeling like an idiot on the quiet. I had no idea something important might have happened.

My name is Rowan Clark and I'm not the same person as I was in that shop, not any more. The rowan is a tree that's meant to protect you from bad things. People made crosses out of it to keep away witches in the days before they knew any better. Maybe my mum and dad named me it on purpose, maybe not, but it didn't do much good. Bad things and my family acted like magnets back then, coming together whatever was in the way.

When I got home with the shopping, I forgot about the negative because there was too much to do. Mum was asleep on the sofa while Stroma watched *Fairly Odd Parents* with the sound off. Stroma's my little sister. She was named after an island off Caithness where nobody lives any more. There used to be people there until 1961 and one of them was someone way back in my dad's family. Then there was just one man in a lighthouse, until they made the lighthouse work without the man and he left too. That's what Stroma and her namesake have in common, getting gradually abandoned.

I made scrambled eggs on toast with cut up oranges and a glass of milk. While we were eating, I asked her how her day was, and she said it was great because she got Star of the Week for writing five sentences with full stops and everything. Being Star of the Week means you get a badge made from cardboard and a cushion to sit on at story time, which is a big deal, apparently, when you're nearly six.

I asked her what her five sentences were, and she said they were about what she did at the weekend. I said, "What did we do?" and she reeled them off, counting them on her fingers.

"I went to the zoo. With my mum and dad. We saw tigers. I had popcorn. It was fun."

Five lies, but I let it slide, and after a minute she met my eye and started talking about something else I couldn't quite make out because her mouth was full of orange. Stroma and I had whole conversations with our mouths full. It was one of the benefits of parentless meals. That and eating with your fingers and having your pudding first if you felt like it.

After supper she did a drawing of a torture chamber while I washed up.

"It's us going swimming," she said, pointing at the rivers of blood and the people hanging from walls.

I said, "We can go on Saturday if you want," which she did and I already knew it.

She asked me to draw a unicorn, and even though it looked more like a rhinoceros and should have gone in the bin, she coloured it pink out of loyalty and called it Sparkle.

When she was all clean and in her pyjamas, we'd read a book and she was feeling sleepy, Stroma asked for Mum. Just like a kid from Victorian times who gets to see a parent in order to bid them goodnight, but the rest of the time has to make do with the staff. I said Mum would be ten minutes because I'd have to wake her up first. I put this lullaby tape on that Stroma listened to every night since forever and I knew she'd probably be asleep before anyone made it up there.

Mum hated being woken up. A cup of tea didn't even scratch the surface of her hatred for it. You could see the world enter her eyes and become fact and pull her back under with the weight of itself. As soon as she was awake she just wanted to go back to sleep again. I knew that we had to be patient, and I do understand that sleep was where she got to pretend her life wasn't crap, but I also think that two live daughters might have been something to stay awake for.

I rubbed her back for a bit and then I said Stroma was waiting.

She brushed me off and got to her feet and said, "What does she want now?" like it'd been her feeding and bathing and entertaining Stroma all evening, not me.

I said, "She just wants a kiss goodnight," and Mum rolled her eyes and moved towards the stairs like her whole body was glued down, like it was the last thing on earth she felt like doing.

I watched her and I thought what I always thought – that the old Mum was trapped inside this new one's body, helpless like a princess in a tower, like a patient on the operating table whose anaesthetic's failed so she can't move or call out or let anyone know. She just had to watch with the rest of us while everything went horribly wrong.

With everybody out of the room and all my jobs done and a moment to think, I remembered the boy in the shop and the negative that wasn't mine. I got it out to have a look. I'd never really seen one before. It was folded over on itself and covered in the dust that lives at the bottom of my bag. It seemed so out of date, shinier on one side than the other, its edges dotted with holes, a clumsy way to carry a picture. I held it up to a lamp.

It's hard to adjust your eyes to something that's dark where it should be light. It was like looking at a sea creature or a mushroom, until I saw it was an open mouth and I was holding it upside-down. The mouth was pale where it should be darkest, towards the back of the throat. That's about all I could see, an open mouth filled with light and two eyes like eyes on fire, the pupils white, the iris shot with sparks against the black eyeballs.

It was a face pushing out light from within, beaming it through the eyes, the open mouth and nostrils, like somebody exhaling a light bulb.

two

I haven't mentioned my brother Jack yet, which is odd because he's the thing most people knew about me then. Wherever I went, being Jack's sister was my ticket in. It was easy. Everyone loved Jack. I didn't have to do anything to make them love me too. It was all taken care of.

How would I describe my big brother to someone who doesn't know him? I could start with nice to look at (my dad's height, my mum's skin). Or clever, because learning new stuff just never seemed hard for him. Maybe funny. When you'd been with Jack for a while, I guarantee your stomach muscles would start to ache. And generous, because he'd give anything to his friends if they needed it.

But I don't want to put anyone off. All of those things are Jack, but not in a smug or annoying way, not so you mind someone else having all the luck. If you ask me, he's one of those people who make a room more interesting when they're in it, who make everyone else wilt just a little when they leave.

There's two years between us and then nearly ten until Stroma, so we were like the first round of kids, the planned ones I suppose.

If I was going to tell someone just one of my Jack stories, it would be his 'Map of the Universe'. I think it came free with *National Geographic*. He'd had it for years, stuck on the inside of his wardrobe door, but no one else had ever really looked at it.

One day Mum was ranting about the mess everywhere and how she couldn't think straight because of everybody's crap around the house. You could hear her coming up the stairs talking to herself about it. She came into Jack's room with a pile of clean laundry. He had most of her coffee cups in there, all in various stages of penicillin. His sheets were balled up on the floor and his mattress was propped against the chest of drawers because he'd just been teaching me how to jump-slide down it. The bin was overflowing (and it stank) and the floor was so littered with books and bits of paper and caseless CDs that it was hard to know where to tread.

"Why," said Mum, "do I bloody bother?" and she looked around, and then down at the ironed clothes she was fool enough to be carrying.

I could feel her slave speech coming on so I tried to blend into the wall.

Jack put his arm around her and said, "Come and look at this, Mum." He stood her in front of the wardrobe, stood behind her with his hands on her shoulders. He was already way taller than her then. When he opened the doors, everything tumbled out like clothing lava. I think there was fruit peel and crisp packets in there too.

Mum sort of bellowed and made fists and screwed her eyes tight shut, and there was this quiet pause where I thought she was going to properly start. But Jack said, "No! No, that wasn't it, that's not what I wanted to show you, honest," and he was laughing and refusing to let her get angry around him. I was so close to that place where laughing is bad and it's impossible not to. I couldn't look at him.

He pointed to the map and said, "This is the

KNOWN UNIVERSE," in a rumbling, half-serious voice like that man who does all the movie trailers.

Mum was still holding the laundry. She rolled her eyes and started to speak, but Jack stopped her. He had the broken aerial of his radio in his hand and he was using it to point at the map like a teacher, like a weather man.

"This tiny dot," he said, "is PLANET EARTH. And that lives in this cylinder here, which is our SOLAR SYSTEM. That's the sun and all the planets, right? You knew that."

Mum's foot was tapping, double-time, like, "Let's get this over with".

"Now this cylinder, our solar system, with the sun and the planets and everything, is *this* tiny dot in this cylinder which is the NEIGHBOUR GROUP." He paused for effect, like he was looking at a class of scientists.

"And the neighbour group is now *this* tiny dot in *this* next cylinder which is a SUPER CLUSTER. Are you getting this?"

There were five or six cylinders altogether and the last one was the KNOWN UNIVERSE.

"The KNOWN UNIVERSE' he said to her over and over again. "THE *KNOWN*."

Mum said, "What does this have to do with anything?"

"Well," Jack said with his hands outstretched and this "love me" look on his face. "How important is a tidy room now, in the scheme of things? Where does it register on the map?"

Mum laughed then and so could we. Jack gave her this big bear hug and she said he was far too smart for his own good. She threw his clean clothes on top of everything else on the floor.

And she said, "You still have to tidy up."

Like I said. One of those people who make a room more interesting when they're in it.

I'm not saying Jack's perfect. I'm not pretending he hasn't wound me up or kicked me too hard or made me eat mud and stuff like that, because of course he has. Maybe all brothers do. It's just that he also looked after me and made me laugh and told me I was cool and taught me things nobody else but your big brother can.

So I miss him.

We all miss him.

We've been missing him for more than two years now. And it's never going to end.

three

Bee would have been in Jack's year. I knew her face, but I'd never spoken to her. She came from somewhere else about a year after he died. I knew nothing about her. The only reason I noticed her that day in the lunch hall was that she was looking at me.

At first I thought she was doing it by accident – that staring-into-space thing where you wake up and realise you've been looking straight at someone and they're wondering why. She was watching me and I was waiting for her to snap out of it, but she didn't. Instead she walked right up to me like I was on my own, and she smiled and looked around and said hello, and then she said, "What was it?" Like that, out of nowhere.

I said, "What was what?" because I didn't have a clue what she was talking about.

Bee said, "The thing he gave you. What did he give you?"

I said, "Who?"

And she said, "The boy in the shop."

I asked her how she knew about it and she said she was behind us all in the queue. I tried to picture the people staring at me in the shop that day, but Bee wasn't one of them.

It was days since then.

"I was there," she said. "I saw the whole thing. He was cute. What was it – his phone number?"

I laughed a bit louder than everyone else and said, "No way, as *if*," and looked at my shoes.

Bee said I'd put up quite a fight and I said, "Well, it wasn't mine."

She said, "What wasn't yours?"

I wasn't sure if I still had the negative on me. I had to dig around in my bag for a while before I found it. She held it up to the strip lighting, this bedraggled little opposite of a picture.

We were quiet for a minute, then Bee said, "Who is it?" and I said, "I don't know."

She said, "Do you think it's a man or a woman?" but I couldn't tell.

She said, "What a weird thing to get given."

I said that was why I'd tried not to take it, because it was obviously a mistake.

"Maybe he saw you drop it," Bee said. But he didn't, because I didn't, and I said so.

She asked me why somebody would make up something like that, what the point would be, and I thought about the boy smiling, about how many people there are out there that you don't know the first thing about. "Takes all sorts," I said, and I held out my hand for it back.

Bee gave it to me and I put it inside a book to smooth out some of the creases.

She asked me what I was going to do with it and I said I hadn't thought. And then the bell went and seven hundred and fifty people started moving for the doors all at once, including Bee, back the way she'd come, without saying goodbye, like our conversation never happened.

* * *

Our house was still a shrine then. Jack was everywhere, smiling out of rooms, watching on the stairs, aged nine and eleven and fourteen, his hair combed and parted, his ears sticking out, grown-up teeth in a kid's mouth. Mum talked to the pictures when she thought she was alone. I heard her. Like one side of an ordinary phone call, like he wasn't dead at all, just moved out and on the other end of the line. The kind of phone call he'd have probably got from her every week the whole of his life. You'd think death could have spared him that.

I never knew what she found to talk about. I was right there and she hardly spoke to me.

Home was quiet like a shrine too. Like the inside of a church, all hushed tones and low lighting and grave faces. There wasn't any Jack noise any more. No loud music, no shouting, no playing the drums on the kitchen table at breakfast, no nothing.

My room had been a landing. When Stroma was born and we needed the space, Dad blocked it off with a new wall and stuck a door in it, but it was too cold for a baby so Stroma got my old room and I moved in. It was tiny, given that it was really just a turning space for somebody using the stairs. There was no radiator and the power came in on an extension from the kitchen, so I was usually cold and I could never lock my door.

Jack's room was on the same floor as Mum's and Stroma's, next to the bathroom. It had two windows and tall bookshelves and an old wooden desk. The walls were a warm grey colour called 'Elephant's Breath'. It was the saddest place in the house, the living, breathing mother ship of everybody's grief. If you were thinking you were getting over Jack and things were nearly back to normal, you'd only have to go in that room and you'd start missing him from the beginning all over again.

Now and then that was just how I wanted to feel.

Sometimes I'd put on some of his music. Sometimes I'd pick up his guitar, but I can still only play the first six notes of *Scarborough Fair* so that never lasted long. I don't even like that song. Usually I'd stretch out on his bed and look at the sky through his windows. That night I sat with my back against the wall and my chin on my knees and I turned the negative over and over between my fingers. I thought about what Bee had said, about what I was going to do next.

Nothing, I thought, and I aimed it into the bin

from where I was sitting and went back to thinking about my brother.

I wasn't sure if Stroma missed Jack, not really. She stuck him at the end of her prayers with Grandad Clark and Great Auntie Helen (who she'd met, like, twice) and the people on *Newsround*, but I reckoned she forgot him almost as soon as he was gone. She hardly ever saw him anyway; maybe at breakfast when he wasn't really awake, or in the car when he'd have headphones on and act like she wasn't there. Jack did loads of nice stuff with Stroma, like taking her to the park or teaching her how to make paper aeroplanes, but I think she was too young to remember. She didn't know him at all. I wonder how she added it up for herself, this stranger in her family dying and turning her family into strangers.

It was me that had to tell Stroma because nobody else had done it. It was the morning after they told me. She had no idea Jack was dead. Everything around her was altered and she was trying so hard not to notice.

She looked up at me and said, "What's the matter with Mummy?" and I said she was sad.

She asked me what Mum was sad about and I said, "Jack's gone," and Stroma carried on humming this little tune and pouring nothing out of a tiny china teapot. Then she said, "Where?" and I said I didn't know. She picked up a cup and saucer and handed it to me. She said, "Blow on it, it's really hot."

I said, "He's dead, Stroma. He's never coming back."

I could feel this weight, this downward pressure in my head, and I thought it was possible I could cave in or implode because I just said that out loud.

Stroma was quiet for a minute, and then she sighed and looked right at me and said, "Can I have something to eat now? I'm starving."

And that was how it started, how I ended up looking after her.

I went into the kitchen to make some toast and there wasn't any bread, not even a crumb. I knocked on the door of Mum's room and got some money and I took Stroma with me to the shop. And all the time I was putting stuff into the basket and working out what we could afford, and saying no to marshmallows, but yes to chocolate biscuits, and planning what we'd have for supper and then breakfast. I didn't have time to lose it. I didn't have time to lie down in the corner shop and scream and beat the floor until my hands bled. I didn't have time to miss Jack. Stroma carried on chattering away and getting excited over novelty spaghetti shapes and finding the joy in every little thing, and it occurred to me even then that she was probably looking after me too.

four

Believe it or not, school was one of my favourite places back then. Everywhere else seemed like hard work, so school was a distraction. I didn't have to worry about where Stroma was. I didn't have to handle Mum. I didn't have to think about the obvious unless I wanted to.

The gap Jack left there got filled pretty quickly by someone else clever and good at running and a bit of a flirt. It was like a day off. Because of course that didn't happen at home. There was no room for anything else. I sometimes thought that if Jack *was* looking down on us all, he'd be feeling majorly hassled, not free to enjoy the afterlife at all.

I think Mum and Dad drove each other crazy with it in the end. They stopped talking altogether about three months before Dad moved out. There was this odd, loaded quiet around them. We kept out of their way.

Maybe they split up because of Jack, because when they looked at each other they only saw him.

Maybe they blamed one another for stuff.

Maybe they were headed that way already. Maybe him dying kept them together a bit longer. I have no idea.

When Dad finally came clean about leaving, he wasn't telling us anything we didn't already know. He'd been staying on sofas for a while, pretending he was at the office, basically avoiding us. He needn't have bothered to pluck up the courage to break old news. Even Stroma had worked that one out, aged five.

He was gone a long time before he was gone, if you know what I mean. And when he left, things just got worse. Because we had him to miss too.

So anyway, school was like a holiday, if you can imagine that.

I don't know how I'd overlooked Bee there before, because after that day she spoke to me, she was the first face I saw in any crowd. It didn't matter who I was with, I'd suddenly be aware that she was around. It was like a special light went on that made her easy to find.

The thing is, once you start looking at Bee you almost have to tell yourself to stop. We aren't so different on paper: same height, same colouring maybe, at a stretch. But Bee has something I don't. Her skin and hair are different shades of the same honey. The way she holds herself is so precise and effortless and graceful I still wonder how she does it. And it isn't just me who thinks that. I see other people watching her all the time, trying to work out how come they aren't put together the same way Bee is.

It was after school the next time I bumped into her and she acted all surprised, but I had this quiet feeling she'd been waiting for me. I had to pick up Stroma and Bee said did we want to get an ice cream or something.

We went to this place at the top of Chalk Farm Road that's been there forever. They sell cones out of a window on the street or you can go in and have sundaes in tall glasses and scoops in a silver cup. Stroma sat on Bee's lap, even though there were about thirty-nine free chairs in there. She was chatting away about some boy in her class called Carl Dean who cut a hole in his shirt on purpose, with scissors, because he needed that exact colour for his collage. She was making us laugh without even trying.

I'd been remembering the birthday party we had there, me and Jack, when he was nine and I was seven. I thought about all the kids who'd come and where they were now, and if any of them remembered Jack or knew he was dead or even minded. I was wondering which chair he had sat on then, and if it was the one I was sitting on now.

It was cool and quiet and empty in the shop. I saw a crowd from my class go past the window, yelling, dancing, drawing attention to themselves. Another day that would've been me, but right then I was glad to be hidden away at a marble table with a girl who said things I hadn't heard ten times before. We finished off Stroma's mint choc chip when she'd had enough. Bee tried to make an origami swan out of her napkin and failed. We looked at the pictures on the wall – signed photos of celebrities nobody'd ever heard of. When the waitress took Stroma off to get more free wafers, Bee asked me if I'd thought any more about the negative.

I hadn't, not at all. It took me a second just to work out what she was on about. She seemed interested, so I said I was going to get it printed, just out of curiosity, to see what it was. I wanted to say the right thing so I could spend more time around her. I knew it would still be in Jack's bin because I was the only one who did the rubbish, Tuesday nights. And that was the only thing in his bin anyway, we never used it. Still, I was thinking I'd just get another negative if that one had somehow disappeared. It's not like she would ever know.

After a bit she said, "If you want to print it I can help you. I know how to do that stuff."

It was nice the way she said it, not pushy, and she said I could bring Stroma, so I said OK.

We went to her house later in the week. Bee lived with her dad and her little brother in a top floor flat on the Ferdinand Estate, with a playground out the front and a view across London. The walkway outside her front door was lined with geraniums and daisies. You could see the Telecom Tower. Bee's dad was called Carl and he had overgrown pale hair and sunken cheeks, and you just knew by looking at him that he played the guitar. Her brother was about two. He was wandering around with a snoopy T-shirt and no pants on, which cracked Stroma up straightaway. He had hair the same colour as Carl's, but all matted and curly.

"I didn't know you had a brother," I said.

"You don't know much about me at all," she said, smiling. "We just met."

We watched the chubby little back of him padding down the hall, Stroma close behind, fussing over him like a sheepdog.

"What's his name?"

"Sonny."

Carl took Stroma and Sonny off to the kitchen to make jam tarts. Stroma couldn't stop giggling. I thought her knees might buckle with the joy of it.

Bee was turning out cupboards in the bathroom. She said it would be much quicker to scan the negative into Photoshop and get an image straight up on screen, but she didn't have a scanner and anyway she printed photos in the bath because it was how Carl had taught her and it was all his equipment. She said the old-fashioned way was better because she liked the not knowing, the time things took to happen. The taps were on and she had her head under the sink. She was talking to me about this thing called the Slow Movement, which seemed to mean baking your own bread instead of nipping out for it to the nearest shop, and making lunch take all day, and getting a boat and a train and another boat instead of flying, because the journey is everything, not just a way of getting from one place to another. She was telling me this stuff I'd never considered and I hadn't even taken my coat off, but I think I got most of it. Bee's brain is as precise and quick and extraordinary as the rest of her, the way she has you look at things.

While I was waiting around, I picked up a book and started leafing through it. One of the photos inside was the first ever photo, Bee said. It was taken more than a hundred and fifty years ago by a Frenchman called Daguerre. She said in those days they had these huge plate cameras and everybody had to sit still for ages if they wanted their picture to come out. They had these special headrests that you clamped yourself in to have your portrait done or else you'd be nothing but a blur.

The photo she showed me wasn't a portrait, or not on purpose anyway. Daguerre had aimed his camera out of the window to take a picture of the street where he lived. It was a busy street in Paris, people everywhere, except in the photo nobody's there, like ghosts in a mirror. The only two people in the picture, the only living things among all the ghosts, are a man having his shoes shined by a boy. Only they had stayed in one place for long enough to become real.

I loved that picture. I looked at them, the two blurry figures in the near distance, and I told myself that sometimes people get noticed and remembered and appreciated without doing anything heroic or extraordinary, without knowing anyone's watching them at all.

The stuff that Bee hauled out of various cupboards was a big sort of microscope, a red light bulb, three trays like you'd plant seeds in, a torch, a pair of tongs and a couple of black bottles. She was setting things out the whole time she was talking to me, laying the trays in the bath, pouring out stuff, screwing the shower head off the bath taps so it ran like a hose, swapping the red bulb for the one that hung bare in the ceiling. She pulled down the blind and closed the wooden shutters, dropping the bar down to keep them closed. Then she bolted the bathroom door and turned on the red light, which took all the colour out of us and the room, apart from itself. Everything went soft around the edges and the whites of Bee's eyes became the same colourless red as her hair and her lips and her skin.

She said, "Where's the negative?" and while I was getting it from my bag, she put her hair up with two pencils. I handed it over and she slid it into the top of the big microscope which she'd balanced on a piece of plywood over the sink. Then she flicked a switch and my negative, nobody's negative, shone A4 size on to a white board below.

I should have recognised it then, but I didn't.

Bee was sizing it up, blocking bits out and squaring them off. "It's so damaged," she said. "We won't get all the scratches out of it."

It was the only source of white light in the room. She was adjusting things, bringing the image in and out of focus so it waved, one minute hazy, the next sharp; like an apparition, like the ghost of a photo, or a photo of a ghost. I couldn't stop looking at the eyes, like those plasma globes that spark inside with lightning when you touch them. Bee was all business, making noises to herself about the quality of the shot, the aperture, stuff that went straight over my head. She said she was going to do a strip test to work out the best exposure time and she started counting, "One, two, three, four – one, two, three, four," four times altogether before she poured some of the liquid into the trays and put the paper into the first tray with her special tongs. The room stank, a sharp sour toxic smell my lungs didn't want to let in.

"Watch this," Bee said, and the paper began to darken and cloud. "It's only a slice of it, maybe a bit of cheek or chin."

She picked it up and dipped it in tray two, trailing it through the liquid again. "That's the fixer," she said. "That stops the photo from disappearing on you later."

I nodded, but she wasn't looking at me. She unlocked the door and slipped out into the bright hallway for a moment. "Ten seconds," she said on her way back in. "Ten seconds should do it."

The ghost came back on and Bee counted to ten, and then the paper went into the developing tray again and I held my breath. I guess I counted to twenty before something started to appear. Bee was right about the waiting bit, the anticipation. My chest was tight and I was taking these quick shallow breaths because of the stench, and everything was focused on this white paper, about to change in the red light.

When it happened, it happened way too fast.

Suddenly, there he was, looking straight up at us

with his hand on his throat and his eyes shining and his mouth wide open in a laugh.

Jack.

The fluid lapped and rippled over his face as it moved in the tray. He looked like he was drowning in it. I was on my knees with my cheek on the cold edge of the bath. I wasn't sure how I got there. I was swallowing and swallowing and my mouth kept flooding with water.

Bee picked my brother up with the tongs and slid him into the fixer. She didn't say a word. Jack looked at me and laughed. He laughed until the fixer was done and while she held him under running water to wash the chemicals off. He laughed while she cleaned up around me and switched the light bulbs back and opened the window.

He laughed the whole time, pegged up on the clothes line, dripping into the bath.

five

When Stroma was smaller, she used to try to see round the corners of things. Every time somebody read her *Babar the Elephant* she'd stop at the page where his mother gets killed and tie herself in knots for a look at the face of the hunter who shot her. I never told her that you can't see all the way round on a flat piece of paper, but she must have found out somehow because she stopped looking.

I reminded myself of Stroma, holed up in Bee's bathroom, searching Jack's photo for things that weren't there. His eyes were pale and glassy, the irises ringed with black, the pupils like pinpricks. They looked like mirrors in the grey of the print. I thought I might see something reflected in them, the way you see things in the back of a spoon or in someone else's sunglasses, but there was nothing there of any use, only the shadow of my own face peering into the shine of the paper.

Bee's dad got me out of there in the end because Sonny needed the loo and he really couldn't wait any longer or things would get messy. Leaving the picture was like leaving a cinema on a sunny day. I didn't know what to do with my eyes because they weren't looking at Jack any more.

Stroma grabbed me in the corridor and talked at a million miles an hour about how she'd rolled out pastry and used special cutters and put only half a spoon of jam in each one and did I want to see them cooking, did I, did I? But I didn't.

Bee gave me a glass of water and sat with me in the sitting room. She looked out of the window, hands in her lap, back dead straight, jaw held tight shut like she was forcing her teeth together. It must have been awkward for her.

I said, "Do you know who that is?" and she nodded.

I said, "How come? From pictures at school?" and she nodded again.

I guess she didn't know what to say either.

I wouldn't have listened if she had. Every sound was suddenly too loud for my ears and I couldn't get my breathing right and I had this overwhelming need to be on my own in the dark, seeing and hearing nothing.

Sonny came into the room with jam all over his hands and his face and his T-shirt. He started to use me like a climbing frame, like I was just more furniture.

"Sorry," Bee said, and she picked him up by his waist and twirled him around and kissed the jam on his nose. "Go and find Papa."

I was numb all over.

I left the negative behind and I took Jack home in an envelope. Mum was in bed and if she heard us coming in, she didn't show it. I opened a tin of soup for Stroma and skipped the bath and read her the shortest book I could find. I promised I'd ask Mum to go and kiss her if she got up. Then I took my brother to my room, sat against the door so no one would get in, and I looked and I looked and I looked.

I've thought about it a lot, how much Jack changed

in the time after he died. Don't ask me how, but he wasn't himself any more.

So what if you couldn't move for school photos and team photos and brushed hair and smiling? None of them were the real him. Jack would *never* have let Mum get those photos out to show people. He'd have burned them if he could. They had fights over it. And his room was the same, but totally different, like a stage set of itself, like a piece in a museum, a fake boy's room. I don't think I ever saw his bed made when he was alive. He let plates and cups collect and fester on his desk for weeks. He stashed food under the bed and he smoked out of the window, even when the wind blew it straight back in so everything smelled of weed and old bananas and his socks, not air freshener and dust and the stopping of time.

When I think of people like Kurt Cobain or River Phoenix or Marilyn Monroe, it seems the most famous thing they ever did was die young. They stopped being real people who took drugs or told lies or went to the loo or whatever. They became saints and geniuses overnight. They became whoever anybody wanted them to be.

It was the same with Jack. He was a saint. We were just the living.

I pictured Mum lying in her room, all absence and silence and skin and bone. This boy she was grieving for, this perfect boy who made her life worth living, who made her forget she had other kids to love – who was he exactly? She loved him and everything, obviously, but I don't recall her worshipping him like that when he was alive. I remember her calling him a little shit and grounding him for borrowing out of her purse. I remember her yelling at him to get up in the morning and stop peeing in the houseplants.

Even Jack would look bad if you compared him to his dead self. It was as if by losing him, she got him back, the son she wanted, the one she imagined having, before Jack was born and his personality got in the way.

Looking at that picture I realised there was something about it that was different to all the other ones plastering the house. His hair didn't look combed or over-shiny. It looked thick and dark and messy, like every day. His skin looked like you could reach out and touch it. It was so detailed, the chicken pox scar on his brow bone, the flush on his cheeks, the way a smile could change his face completely if he meant it. There was a brightness about him. He was happy, not acting that way in front of a cheesy backdrop.

It was off duty. It was real. It was the person I was missing.

It was the Jackest picture of Jack I'd ever seen.

six

There's no need to go through all the ways I tried to make sense of my own brother's face showing up like that. None of them worked anyway. A stranger had given me something I'd never seen before that turned out to be mine. How was I supposed to feel? How could it be mine if I'd never seen it?

If I had no idea something existed, how could I manage to drop it? I checked the lining of my coat, the insides of my bag, the pockets of everything, and I didn't find anything else I'd never seen before.

And this boy who gave it to me. I tried to remember what he looked like. Dark hair, dark eyes, I had a few details, but I couldn't see him clearly. I wasn't even sure

I'd recognise him again. Did he know what he was doing or was it a coincidence? Which of those was worse?

I'm not a fan of coincidence and fate and all that. It makes me feel like there's no point doing anything if you can't change things, if you can't be even a tiny bit in charge. Plus I realised that if there was coincidence, there was also *anti*-coincidence, the thing that only just *never* happens by the skin of its teeth, and because you're not expecting it, you have no idea that it almost did.

Everywhere I went, I pictured him just leaving, disappearing round a corner or about to arrive, but only when I'd gone. It wasn't a good feeling. It tied me up like a ball of string in a cartoon.

I didn't show anyone else in my family the picture, not Mum or Dad or Stroma. I kept it to myself, hid it in the dark far corner underneath my bed where I could reach for it at night and where nobody else ever bothered to go. It had found me so it was mine. That's what I figured.

Every so often, Mum had to go to the doctor to prove she was taking her medicine and not selling it on the black market. She must have cost the NHS a pile of money with all the pills she was on so they probably needed to make sure she was worth it. I swear she had the wrong prescription because the only thing different about Mum since she'd started taking it was that she'd got thinner. The bones in her hands and face were clearer than they used to be, like the ground coming back under melting snow.

I had a list of questions for the doctors, like whether they knew Mum was bereaved and not overweight, and if she ever actually said a word to them because she was pretty much silent at home. I wanted to ask them what happened next, but they couldn't talk to me because I was a minor and it was all a big secret.

They didn't know that I came with Mum every time because without me she wouldn't even get there. It flew under their radar that I was the one making sure she arrived in one piece and behaved herself, not the other way round.

The waiting room was jammed with bored kids and posters about sexually transmitted diseases. There were polite notices everywhere that said if you punched any of the receptionists you were in big trouble. Mum was sitting next to me with her eyes closed and her nose and mouth buried in a scarf. It wasn't even cold. Stroma was doing her best to play with three bits of Lego and a coverless book.

When they called Mum's name over the loudspeakers, she ignored it. I watched her trying to disappear inside her own clothes.

Stroma said, "Mummy, that's you," and started pulling at her. The receptionists were watching.

The doctor's voice came on again: "Jane Clark to Room 5."

Stroma managed to pull Mum's sleeve right over her hand, so her arm stayed somewhere inside her coat, lolling against her body, inert like the rest of her, hiding.

"Come on, Mum," I said, pulling her towards her feet by her other hand. "You have to get up and see the doctor."

We looked ridiculous, we must have done. Two kids trying to force a grown woman to move. In the end, somebody muttered into a phone and a doctor came down to take Mum upstairs.

"It's not working," I said to him. "Whatever you're doing isn't working!" And my voice got louder and angrier in the hush of the room. I sat back down and waited for people to stop staring. Stroma climbed on to my lap and put one arm round my neck. Part of me wanted to push her off and walk out. The other part kissed the top of her head and looked around.

And that's when I saw him, the boy. He was sitting on a bench opposite and to my left, in the corner, and he was watching us.

Stroma must have felt me tense every muscle because she looked up at me and said, "What?"

I shook my head and said, "Nothing," but I didn't take my eyes from him because I couldn't. He was wearing a black top with the hood up. He didn't move when I saw him. He didn't flinch or even blink. He didn't look surprised. He smiled and I remembered the chip in his tooth. My face felt tight and clumsy, like someone else's, so I didn't smile back. I just rested my chin on Stroma's head and carried on looking.

I knew I had to ask him about Jack's picture. I knew this was my chance. I was working out what to say when the woman at the desk called out, "Harper Greene? Harper Greene? Can you fill in this form, please?" And the boy stood up.

At the same time, Mum came out, empty-faced, eyes dead ahead, and Stroma jumped off my lap. They headed for the door. I couldn't let either of them cross the road without me.

"It's just your address," the woman with the clipboard was saying to the boy. "You haven't put one down."

He had an accent, American maybe. I hadn't remembered that. "Market Road," he said. "Number 71."

And he looked straight at me when he said it.

Market Road is not the sort of road you stroll down lightly if you're a girl. I said that to Bee as soon as she started her go-and-meet-this-Harper-Greene campaign on me. I reminded her that most of the girls walking down there were working pretty hard to pay off their drug debts.

She said, "Don't walk then. Go on your bike if it makes you feel better."

We were sitting under a tree in Regent's Park, watching Sonny and Stroma fill a bin bag with conkers. Stroma liked being the oldest for once. She was ordering Sonny about like her life depended on it, doing quality control on his offerings, and he didn't seem to mind one bit.

I'd been talking about the photo. I'd been telling Bee some stuff about Jack. I said, "I just don't get how it could show up like that out of nowhere. It's like he's trying to tell me something. And I never thought I'd hear myself talk crap like that."

"Maybe the boy knows, maybe he doesn't. I just think you need to ask him."

"I'm not going," I said. Bee shrugged and stared up through the leaves. "I mean it," I said. "I'm not going."

"You're chicken," she said quietly, almost like she didn't want me to hear. "You're being a coward."

I said she was right. I said I was a coward, a sensible one. Isn't that what you're told to be when you're growing up and you're a girl? Don't go to chat rooms, don't go out alone, don't trust anyone, don't talk to strangers and don't meet them, ever. I'd had it drummed into me so hard, safety, safety, super safety, and I'd soaked it all up like a sponge. I hardly ever crossed a road unless the green man told me to. I didn't sleep right if the door was unlocked or I knew there was a window open somewhere. I carried my keys, stuck out sharp between my knuckles, if I was out after dark; even if it was still daytime, even if it was just the walk home from school in winter. So why the hell would I send myself to that part of town to look for some strange boy I had no reason to trust?

I told Bee about the time me and Stroma were walking down the canal. We came round the corner on an empty path and ahead of us was a man, fishing. He was dressed like he'd seen too many war films, combats and dog tags and mirrored shades. He had a bare, bright white, too-bony chest and instantly I didn't trust him. I got this picture of him in my head, slicing open a fish with a big glinting knife. I grabbed Stroma's hand and ran back the way we'd come, looking behind me to see if he was chasing us, dragging my poor sister through nettles and dog shit. And he wasn't, poor guy; he didn't do anything.

"He was just fishing," I said. "But I didn't think so because I'm paranoid. That's my point."

Bee listened and she said she got it, the whole stranger-danger thing. She said it was good to be careful. She also said there was a big difference between being careful and being shit-scared of everything. She said, "Being afraid all the time is no way to live. What's it going to be? A bomb? A dark alley? Some boy who picked up a photo off the floor? Do you think you can stop bad things happening to you just by fearing them?"

"No," I said.

"Then why are you bothering?" she said. We were quiet for a minute, then she said, "He's not some fifty-year-old bloke pretending to be a teenage girl on the Internet, Rowan."

"I know that," I said. "But he still might be an axe-wielding maniac."

"Whatever," Bee said. "He might also be a cool person. If you insist on never trusting all the people you haven't met before, just because you've never met them, your world's going to be a very lonely place."

"I've got enough friends," I said. "I've got loads."

Bee laughed and said that was the saddest thing she'd ever heard. She changed the way she was sitting and turned to me. "How would you like to die?"

I said I wouldn't like to at all and she laughed and said I had to choose a way, I couldn't say that.

"How would *you* like to die?" I asked her.

She said, "I want to fall out of an aeroplane," and I said, "What? You're joking! Why?"

She said that she'd want to really know her time was

up and there was no possibility of hope, so she could kind of throw herself at it and dive straight in. "Plus," she said, "I'd be flying."

I stared at her with my mouth open. *To be that brave*, I thought.

Bee said, "So, what about you?"

I didn't want to say now. I felt like a fool.

"In my sleep, when I'm old. Nice and peaceful," I said. "I thought everyone did."

"You surprise me, Rowan," Bee said. "The shit you deal with. I think you're way braver than that."

We sat under the tree and I thought about it. Mum and Dad moved us to a school because they thought it was better. They moved house to keep us safer. They gave us swimming lessons and cycle helmets and self-defence classes and a balanced diet. They paid our phone bills so we'd never run out of credit in a crisis. They promised us five grand on our twenty-first birthdays if we never smoked.

And still one of us died.

What can I say? Death is just one of those things that you can work out a thousand different ways of avoiding, but you're going to meet head on regardless.

I looked at the side of Bee's beautiful face under the shadow of the leaves. I thought about the things she knew and the places she'd been and the books she'd read. I thought about how much better I felt just for knowing her. I thought about her and Carl and Sonny and their front door with the flowers outside. I thought it couldn't hurt to be a little more like her. What was the point of being afraid of things before they happened? Why not wait till they were on top of you and then deal with them?

"You're right," I said. "You're always right."

"So do it," Bee said. "What have you got to lose?"

Which is how I found myself at half-past four on a grey afternoon, getting rained on and looked at, cycling not too slow and not too quick, counting down doorways on Market Road. Bee was looking after Stroma. That was the final brick in her house of getting Rowan to do it.

seven

Market Road was long and the buildings were fairly spaced out. There was a massive estate set well back from the road, six huge blocks with cheerful names like Ravenscar and Coldbrooke. I tried to look purposeful (but not businesslike) and I kept going. I was beginning to wonder if 71 even existed. And then I passed it. It was on a corner, a smashed up, boarded up, covered-in-bird-shit old pub. The signs had been painted out in black and the number 71 was daubed on the front door in white gloss. It didn't look like anybody but the pigeons lived there. There was no way I was going in.

I stopped at the kerb a little way past and turned round. I was balancing my bike with one foot on the ground, looking for my mobile to call Bee and tell her it was a big nothing, when I saw the van parked outside the building, round the corner. It was an old ambulance with long double doors at the back and stripy curtains. The driver's door was open on to the pavement and Harper Greene was sitting there, his seat pushed back, both feet up on the windscreen. He was reading a book. For maybe ten seconds I stood quite still. His hair was cut so short you could see the skin beneath, the shape of his skull. I liked his face. I could break it down and say his nose was straight and his eyes were brown and all that, but it wouldn't work like his face worked, together all at once. Like Jack used to say when something good happened, you had to be there. I watched the slow movements of his breathing, his quick eyes scanning the page. I breathed in hard and I thought, *What would Bee do?*

When I got off my bike and started pushing it towards him, he looked round and smiled like he'd been expecting me. Then he got up and disappeared over the back of his seat and opened the double doors at the back, as if that was the way you received guests in an old ambulance, like everyone knew that was the way you answered the door.

We said hello at the same time. I wasn't doing a great job of looking him in the eye.

"I'm Harper," he said.

I nodded and said, "I know," but I was supposed to say, "I'm Rowan," so I did, when I finally realised.

"Pleased to meet you," he said, and he put his hands in his pockets, I guess instead of shaking mine.

"Is this where you live?" I said.

"At the moment," he said. "I move around."

"Market Road?" I said.

And he laughed and said, "Yeah, very scenic, but the parking is free."

I asked him where he was from. He said, "New York. You?"

"Around here," I said. I pointed at the pub. "Who lives in there?"

"Oh, no one," he said. "I guess they moved out a while ago. It's wrecked in there."

"I like your ambulance."

He smiled. "Me too." He said he got it "from a guy" for hardly anything because the guy was going back to New Zealand and he wanted it to have a good home. It was strange, Harper talking about stuff while the thing I wanted him to talk about just waited.

"Do you want to come in?" he said.

"I don't think so."

I was still holding on to my handlebars. He asked me if I was worried about my bike. I shook my head. I said, "Why did you give it to me?"

"What? The thing you dropped?"

"I didn't drop anything."

"I saw you," he said, and he was smiling, like he couldn't believe I was arguing with what he knew to be true. "You dropped it on the doorstep of the shop and I picked it up."

I told him I thought it was a joke at first. "I thought you just gave stuff to people for a laugh. I thought you were trying to show me up in front of everyone."

He said that would be too weird and we both laughed, but only a little.

"What's weird," I said, "is that I've never seen that photo before. But it does belong to me."

He asked me what I meant and I said, "It's of somebody I know."

"Isn't that because you dropped it, because it was yours?" He smiled and held his hands out in front of him to say, why are we still talking about this?

"I don't know," I said. "Maybe I did, but I still haven't worked out how."

"I don't get why that's hard. People drop things all the time."

I got the feeling he was beginning to wonder about me; about my sanity, I mean. I said, "It's a picture of my brother, and my brother is dead." I hoped really hard he wasn't going to say something cushiony.

"God, I'm sorry," he said, and then, "Can I get you a drink?"

Part cushion, part nothing, which was fine.

I propped my bike against a wall and sat down in the doorway of the ambulance. While Harper was lifting the lid off the little hidden cooker and filling a kettle by pressing his foot down on the floor, I said, "Do you see why it's weird? That I never saw it before and you found it and it's of him?"

He said he really hadn't meant to freak me out. He said, "I guess you owned it without knowing."

"Yeah, but even that's doing my head in. I wouldn't have it and then forget about it. It's a really amazing photo."

"It's a mystery," he said. "I get it. You want to solve it."

We sat on the floor of the van with the back doors open and our feet on the ground. The tea was some spicy, gingery thing that came out of a packet covered in proverbs, but it tasted quite good.

He said, "Have you always lived around here?"

"Norf London girl," I said and he laughed.

"Upstate New York boy."

I didn't know what to say about New York. I'd never been there. I didn't know what upstate meant. I said, "Wow," or something just as vacant and then I asked him how old he was. Eighteen last August, three months older than Jack. I said, "How did you get it together to do all this, leave home and travel around and everything?"

"I always wanted to do it," he said. "The world's so big, you got to start early. I wanted to get moving, get away."

"Get away from what?" I said, and he shrugged.

"Everything and nothing. I just wanted to move."

I was rolling a bit of gravel around under my shoe. "Everything," I said. "I'd like to get away from that too."

There was a football match going on in the sports fields opposite. We could just see the players' heads bobbing around above the level of the wall.

"Just so you know," he said, "it turns out not to be possible."

"What's that supposed to mean?"

"Oh, I don't know. You're always gonna be you, doesn't matter where in the world you are."

I thought of Jack's TOO DEEP WARNING LIGHT, this thing he used to say when anyone got a bit self-help on him, a bit road-less-travelled. It made me smile. If I'd known Harper better, I'd have told him what was so funny. I asked him where he'd been so far.

"I flew from New York to Paris. I wanted to go by boat, but it costs way too much. I wanted to be in the middle of an ocean. Nothing but water for weeks; see if I went crazy. Maybe another time. I stayed with a friend in Montparnasse for a while. Then I got the train here. I haven't been doing this too long. I'm pretty new at it."

"Where are you going next?"

"I just got here, so nowhere for a month or so. I want to go to Scotland and Norway and Spain and, well, wherever. Plus I've got to work when I can, when the money's low. We'll see. What about you?"

"Oh, nothing, nowhere," I said. "I haven't done anything yet." He seemed to find that funny so I didn't tell him it wasn't a joke.

He asked me about Mum. I wished he hadn't seen her that day, in the doctor's. I told him she wasn't like that really, which was a lie. I told him they were adjusting her medication and it was just a question of waiting. I stuck up for her because I knew I should, but I wouldn't have believed a word of it if I was him.

He said, "Was that your sister with you?" and I said yes, and what with the Jack fall-out and my dad going part-time on us, I'd pretty much been left in charge. I told him that my friends were getting bored with me because I couldn't hang around too much, and if I did, it was with a six-year-old in tow. I heard myself grumbling and complaining to this person I'd just met, and I was telling myself, "Stop it! Be funny, be cool. Stop doing this."

But it was true and I couldn't make it leave my head if it was there. While my friends were thinking about what their jeans looked like in their boots, I was wondering how much milk there was in the fridge. When they talked about make-up and boys, I heard laundry and CBeebies. I said, "I'm not much of a picnic to know any more."

Harper stood up and poured the rest of his tea on a straggly plant growing out of the kerb. He said he'd be the judge of that, if it was OK by me.

At about half six I stood up and started fixing the lights on to my bike. I wasn't ready to leave at all. Harper said, "Did you want to stay and eat? I'm a not bad cook."

"I can't. I have to get my sister. I have stuff to do."

I thanked him for the photo. I said, "I've no idea where it came from, but I suppose it's mine and I'm glad to have it."

"You're welcome," he said. "I'm glad it was you."

I wheeled out on to the darkening road, past the sad cases and the kerb crawlers and the football players and Harper waving at me until he was out of sight.

I couldn't stop smiling.

When I got to Bee's, she said didn't I get her messages, that she'd sent three while I was gone. "Even I started to wonder if he was an axe-wielder when I didn't hear back."

I hadn't checked my phone. I didn't think she'd be worrying. "He lives in an ambulance," I said because I knew she'd like that. "He's from New York."

"Did you like him?"

"Yes, I liked him."

"What did you talk about?"

"Not much. I wasn't there that long."

"Yes, you were," Bee said. "You've been gone nearly three hours."

"I suppose so. He's travelling. He's funny. He's very cool."

"Told you," she said.

"I liked him a lot."

"How did it go?"

"How did what go?"

"Did you talk about the thing, the picture? I thought that's why you went."

I said we had, but not really. "I don't know. Maybe I did drop it. I must have done."

"And you're going to see him again."

I shrugged, like it wasn't something I was in charge of. Even if I did want to hang out with Harper, there was Stroma to think about. I said that to Bee with my hands over Stroma's ears while she wriggled to get free. I said it wasn't so easy making plans with a kid in tow.

Bee raised her eyebrows at me. She said I didn't have to make life so complicated. She said she'd look after Stroma any time. She said, "Not everyone minds being around little kids."

I stood there and I thought about my friends who'd rather be seen dead than out with my sister. I thought about the times they'd said couldn't I just leave her somewhere, anywhere, and come out with them. I thought about the times I'd wished I could. I felt like a bad person.

I said, "Are you always right?"

"Course not," she told me. "I'm just never wrong."

When I got Stroma home from Bee's, it was cold and all the lights were off, like there was nobody in. Mum was on the sofa in the dark. I hung up our coats and Stroma's book bag. I rinsed out her lunchbox. She sat at the kitchen table, drawing, while I boiled water for pasta and scraped the fur off the pesto sauce without her noticing. We jumped around when something good came on the radio. Stroma climbed up on the table and put her heart and soul into it. Neither of us mentioned the lack of a parent in the room. Neither of us expected a kiss or a smile or a cup of hot chocolate. Neither of us said this is not what other families do every evening. I guess we were used to it by then.

There were two messages from Dad on the answer phone. That was about all he got out of Mum, her recorded we're-not-in-right-now voice from months and months ago. It was also the closest he got to parenting during the week because he worked long hours and always forgot to call us when we were actually there. He said things like, "Don't forget to brush your teeth, Stroma" and "I hope you're studying, Rowan" and "I hope my two best girls are behaving" and we rolled our eyes and carried on with whatever we were doing. It was pathetic really.

I remember the day Mum and Dad announced they were going to have another baby. That was when they still liked each other. We were having breakfast. I was trying not to think about them having sex.

Jack said, "Please, I'm eating," and I sniggered through my cornflakes and we got sent upstairs. Clearly they didn't see the funny side of getting pregnant at forty.

Jack said, "Do you think they're replacing us because we're not cute any more?" He was sitting on the floor, almost twelve, filling the place up with his legs. He was so big suddenly, I thought, *God, maybe they are*.

When Jack and I were little, Mum and Dad were always doing stuff with us. She'd be sitting on the sofa waiting when we got home from school. I thought that's what she did all day, sat and waited for us. He built spaceships and palaces out of cereal packets and egg boxes. She made me spiral jam sandwiches by rolling the bread into tubes and then slicing them up. He made curries so hot our eyes streamed and water tasted like fire.

We felt like the centre of the universe, I guess because we were the centre of theirs.

With Stroma they were the same. Everything was always covered in icing or sequins or paint. Dad found her a bike at the dump and restored it so it looked brand new. He took her for a ride every evening when he got in, even when he was dead tired, even if it was just round the block. Mum made her a fairy outfit one Christmas and stayed up till two in the morning hand-stitching pink ribbons on to the wings. They made treasure hunts and dance routines and gingerbread men. They never stopped. Jack and I called them the kids' TV presenters, and laughed at their tracksuit bottoms and the paint in their hair. We said they should have more self-respect and act their age. We were just jealous because we weren't the centre of things any more. We were just joking. We were just mean.

The day Stroma was born, when we went in to see

her, Mum said it was astonishing how much love there was in the human heart. She said she thought we'd filled it, me and Jack, but here was a whole-nother-room with Stroma's name on the door.

They must have lost the key. Because now I was the one who spent hours picking playdough off the sofa and toys off the floor. It was me who discovered the instant healing powers of a plaster and how many peas Stroma would tolerate at any one meal. I did the hugging and the singing and the bedtime stories. It wasn't Mum or Dad who skipped down the street yelling, "We're going on a Bear Hunt! We're going to catch a BIG one!" any more. It was me.

But I was never as good at it as them. And I didn't want to be doing it, not all the time, not just because there was no one else, and that must have showed. I wasn't Mum and Dad, and when Stroma kicked, off you knew it wasn't just about her swimming kit or the bath mat from her dolls' house or the brown bit on a banana. It was because everything had caved in on top of her and she'd had enough.

I knew already there was no such thing as a normal family. You might think you've got one, but something always happens to prove you wrong. There were kids at school worse off than us, way worse, that's what I kept telling myself. And I knew my parents were good people. It wasn't their fault something bad happened to them.

But after Jack died, they protected themselves by refusing to love us, the kids who had dying still to do. And it fell to us to keep ourselves alive until somebody remembered we were there.

eight

The next day we were sitting in the canteen, me and Bee, watching some of the boys from her class have this food fight. She said, "How are they doing that without getting a hair out of place? Is there that much gel in there?"

I laughed and said, "Jack used to have a thing about some of the girls here too."

"What thing?" she said.

"He used to rant about the taste of lip gloss and the fact they spent all their time looking at themselves in reflective surfaces. He used to make me laugh so hard. I had to promise never to be one of them."

"Well, you're not," Bee said. "And neither am I." She

got up to put her stuff in the bin, and I watched her and so did everyone else. I so wished that Jack was still around to meet Bee. It was like a sudden ache in my side, that never happening. He'd have liked her as much as I did. I wanted to tell her that, but I didn't know how to say it, so I said nothing.

"What are you up to tonight?" she asked while I was searching in my bag for the homework I couldn't remember doing.

"Cooking dinner, giving Stroma a bath, putting her to bed and hiding in my room," I said, counting things off on my fingers, letting my thumb hang down.

"Why don't you two stay at mine?" she said. "Carl won't mind."

"Yeah, and it would give my mum a break," I said, trying to make it sound funnier than it was.

Bee said, "What's the thing with your mum?"

"It's a 'she's never going to get over her son dying' thing."

She asked if Mum was sick.

"I don't know," I said. "If she was sick, then the medicine would work, I suppose. I think she's just the saddest person ever."

"Oh, God," Bee said. "Imagine how she must feel."

I said she didn't leave a lot to the imagination. I said she made it pretty clear.

Bee looked at me like she was working something out. "Are you pissed off with her?"

"Not a lot of point in that," I said. "There's no one to be pissed off with. She's not in there."

After school I phoned Mum on my mobile. She didn't answer of course, but I left a message, with Bee's phone number, just in case she needed anything. I felt funny about leaving her for the night, like she was my kid or something, like she should have a babysitter. I said to call me if she wanted us home, and I almost wished she would, but I knew she'd probably much prefer a quiet night in without us. I knew she'd barely notice we were gone.

I watched Stroma clinging on to Bee like glue on the walk home. I hoped Bee wasn't claustrophobic.

Stroma stopped dead in the street because she didn't have her teddy or her pyjamas. I nearly piled into the back of her.

Bee said, "You can wear one of my T-shirts."

"Can I use your toothbrush as well or will that be

germs?" Stroma asked. Bee said she thought her toothbrush was safe, but that Sonny's would be a better fit. Stroma said, "What about my mouth though?" Bee sniffed her breath and said she thought that was safe too. It was such a relief, watching someone else take care of my sister.

Sonny was crying when we got there. We could hear him through the door. As soon as he saw us, he started crying even harder. Carl was looking at Bee like it had been going on for too long and he didn't know what to do.

"I've got it, Dad," Bee said. She put her arms out for Sonny and he climbed into them. She took him out through the open front door, down the walkway. His arms were round her neck, fingers laced together through her hair. He was still bawling. Stroma and I were left in the hallway with Carl, who looked like the last thing on earth he needed was two more people in the house. I got this hollow feeling, like staying was going to be a really bad idea and I'd have to start letting Stroma down gently.

"Is it a bad time?" I asked. Stroma groaned, this sort of why-did-you-say-that? noise, like it would be all my fault if we couldn't stay now.

"Oh, he's in a mood, that's all," Carl said, rubbing his ears as if Sonny's noise had got right in there and wouldn't come out. "Bee's good with him when he's like that. He gets sick of me."

He asked if we wanted a drink or a snack or something. He said to Stroma, "You've been at work all day, you must be *pooped*," instantly becoming her funniest person in the world ever.

I watched Bee and Sonny, swaying together. She was talking into his hair, he was playing with hers, still yelling his head off. I wondered where their mum was.

Bee went up and down the walkway for ages and when she came back in, Sonny was asleep on her shoulder. She put him on the sofa without waking him up. Carl said, "Thanks, kid. I was running out of ideas."

Bee shrugged and said, "*Nada*, Dad. Glad to be of service."

Stroma sat with Sonny like she was Florence Nightingale or someone, twitching at his covers, sighing over his cheeks and eyelashes and the rise and fall of his little chest. Acting like he was the cutest thing she ever saw, all the time only four years older than him.

"Has he been all right?" Bee said. "He feels hot."

"A bit moody; he's getting a cold."

I asked if me and Stroma should go. I didn't want to be any trouble.

"No, don't," said Carl. "No, it's great you're here. I'll make some supper before his lordship wakes up. You two do whatever. Come and help me, Stroma. Be my sous-chef."

They disappeared to the kitchen and we stayed where we were, watched Sonny sleeping like he was TV.

"He's lovely," I said.

"He's gorgeous."

I felt bad for moaning so much about Stroma, for making her sound like hard work. I thought, *I bet Bee helps out a load and does it better than me and never goes on about it.* I said something about her being such a good person.

"You're just making stuff up," she said. "What makes me better than you? What are you on about?" She was laughing.

"Well, you're nice about everyone. You never complain."

"I just don't do that out loud. You should be inside my head."

"Are you a monster in there?" I said.

Bee looked dead serious. Funny serious. She narrowed her eyes. "You have no idea."

It cracked me up.

"Was Jack a good person?" she said. "Do you mind me asking?"

"I don't mind at all. I like talking about him. You know that."

"OK, so was he a good person the way you say I am or whatever?"

"He was the best person," I said, and I did a really good job of smiling. "Everyone knew that. He was always helping someone out. Friends that is, not Mum and Dad so much I suppose, but he'd do anything for his friends."

"Who were his friends?" Bee asked.

"Oh, there was Melly who lived down the road, and Pete and Oscar from your class, except Pete's left now, hasn't he? He hung out with them mostly." Melly and Pete and Oscar who tried their best, but didn't know what to say to me when Jack was gone. They didn't have a clue.

"I like Oscar," Bee said. "He doesn't say much, but when he does it's funny."

"I miss him," I said. "Jack, I mean."

"I know you do," she said, sitting behind me, plaiting my hair.

Stroma and Carl made rice with broccoli and tomatoes and fish fingers, enough for everyone. Sonny woke up and clung to Carl and ate like a horse. After supper, Bee took him for a bath and Carl played the shape game with me and Stroma. You draw a random shape and the next person has to turn it into something with a different-coloured felt-tip. Bee joined in too, and Sonny, dripping and shiny from the bath, drew on his own legs and set Stroma off laughing again. Everyone was busy making a six-year-old happy, which made a change from it being just me.

At seven-thirty, Carl took Sonny to bed with a bottle and I read Stroma a story on the sofa. She curled herself up under the quilt, put her thumb in her mouth and started playing with my hair like she used to do with Mum before. After a bit I untangled myself and kissed her on the forehead.

She said, "Can we stay here tomorrow as well?"

Later, Bee and Carl and I were doing the washing-up. We were humming the same tune and doing a kind of dance around each other just to get things done in the tiny kitchen. I didn't know where anything went because there weren't any cupboards. The battered wooden filing cabinet with the radio on top was the last place I expected them to keep plates and cups and saucepans. The cutlery lived in the top left of a chest of drawers, the same sort you put your underwear in. I think jam and honey and stuff went in the right. Whatever was left seemed to live on the table. It was much nicer than those kitchens with plastic cupboards lining the walls and a place for everything. It was much more fun than washing up at home.

When it was as tidy as it was going to be, Carl said, "Time for some sugar," and he started rolling a joint. Bee let her head drop back and said something to the ceiling about being the teenage daughter of a teenager.

"You're not having any," Carl said.

Bee said, "I know," and I held my hands up in the air to say I wasn't interested either.

Jack used to smoke grass. Mum got cross because he'd stop finishing his sentences and eat everything in the house, but really she was relieved he was doing it at home and not in some bus shelter where she couldn't find him. Dad thought she was way too easy on him. He said Jack's room might as well be the bus shelter once all his friends found out you could smoke there, but that never really happened. Maybe once or twice when they were out.

Anyway, Carl smoked and it stank out the kitchen, and then he started making a packed lunch for Stroma.

I said, "I can do that tomorrow morning."

He looked at me. "You know what? It's your night off. Go and watch a movie upstairs or something."

I asked if I could have a bath and Bee went to run me one. When I got there, she'd lit candles and used bubbles and suddenly I felt like Stroma must have done all evening: taken care of. "What would I do without you?" I said, and I really meant it.

"What you've been doing," Bee told me. "Getting on with it. It's what we all do."

Stroma woke up in the night and forgot where she was. She climbed into my sleeping bag and then went straight back to sleep, leaving me with a few centimetres of space and a chance to watch the dawn.

Jack used to sleep badly. When we were younger, he'd shake me awake and say, "It's OK, Rowan, you had a bad dream. I'll look after you."

I always knew it wasn't me who'd been dreaming. I also knew he didn't want to lose face, so I never said anything. I used to lie awake with him snoring in my bed too.

The sky changed from dark to light so slowly I didn't notice it happening and suddenly it was morning. Stroma stretched her little body out and opened her eyes, and that was it; she was wide awake and moving at the speed of sound, filling the place with her questions and her chitchat and her singing. I moved over into the warm space she'd left behind and closed my eyes, feeling that thing sleep does around the edges when you're ready to fall back into it. I could hear Sonny burbling away to someone upstairs, the loo flushing at the end of the hall, Stroma opening the sock drawer in the kitchen. Then I forced myself out of there and into my clothes and the making of breakfast.

Carl said he could take Sonny to the childminder and Stroma to school on his way to work, so I got to go with Bee, on time for once.

"God, Carl's cool," I said while we were waiting for the bus.

"You can say that again." Bee smiled at me. "He's very rare."

"What's he do?"

"He works in a school in Hackney, two or three days a week. He hangs out with all the kids the teachers can't deal with any more. He's their friend. He says he doesn't like teachers either. The rest of the time he's with Sonny."

We stood there for a bit, looking down the road at where the bus should be. "Where's your mum?" I said, and I hoped she didn't mind.

Bee said, "Oh, she's not part of it really. She was young, like my age, when she had me. She's been back a few times, but never for long. She gave Dad a lot of grief."

"What about Sonny?" I said. "He must miss her."

She shrugged. "No. He's better off, I reckon."

I felt like I was prying. I said I was sorry.

"I see my mum now and then," Bee said. "She's pretty wild. She's like an artist's model and a professional hippy, and right now she's in Madrid, cooking macrobiotic food for this insane writer. She's been there two years. I don't mind."

She smiled at me, like she'd said this stuff a thousand times and she was bored of hearing it. "Don't be sorry, because I'm not. Carl took me to India when I was nine. We lived in this community in Wales for a while. He taught me how to take pictures and grow vegetables, and he's into homeopathy and he can speak Italian and…"

"OK," I said. "Sorry was so the wrong word. I'm not sorry."

Except I was, because I felt like never going home again.

nine

Stroma and I were on our way to the little playground after school the next time I saw Harper. We had fish and chips and about forty-five sachets of ketchup in a bag. It was a thing we did sometimes on a Friday to celebrate the end of the week. I wanted to invite Bee, but she was off somewhere with Sonny and Carl. And besides, I noticed Bee mainly ate tofu and salads and bean sprouts. I didn't think supper out of greasy paper in a chill wind would be her thing.

I saw the ambulance parked and I said, "Come on, Stroma, let's go and see a friend of mine."

Harper wasn't there. I picked Stroma up and we looked through the windows at the way he lived. The cupboards had doors that stayed shut and there were little lips on all the shelves so the cups didn't fall out when you went round a corner. There was a book box with a clear front on it so you could read the spines without finding them strewn across the floor. There was a map tacked to the wall, and some photos. There was a larder and a fridge and space to store pillows and blankets and clothes. Stuff had a double life. The back seat was a double bed (and so was the roof). The cooker was a desk. The table came apart and slid in behind the driver.

I know it like the back of my hand now, but I'll never forget being outside with Stroma that time, looking in. It was as good as another world to both of us.

When Harper came back, we were still standing there with our noses pressed against the glass. I was scared to get in because I thought I might not want to get out again. That was what Stroma did, climb in and jump out again, climb in and jump out. She picked dandelions and buttercups in the square, and Harper put them in an egg cup on the table. The whole place stank of fish and chips.

"You moved," I said.

"For a couple of days," he said. "Someone will be on the phone to complain by tomorrow."

He said the people round there were used to being so rich and powerful that they thought they could get anything done. He said he met this guy who worked on the council. They got a letter from the local residents complaining about the seagulls flying inland and making too much noise and crapping on their property. The council wrote back telling them to club together and buy a kestrel.

I said, "You know what? They probably did."

I asked him why he was in London when he could be anywhere. He said he wasn't sure how far the ambulance would go, he hadn't tried it out yet. "And anyway, I'm a tourist, remember?" he said. "I love London. Just because I could leave doesn't mean I want to. I only just got here."

I asked him what was so great about it. I only knew my square mile. I only knew our schools, the park, the shops, our house and the roads between, all dog shit and litter and bookies.

"There's so many people from somewhere else, so many languages spoken here every day. It's exciting, isn't it? It's like travelling without going anywhere, the places you can get to in this city."

Harper said it wasn't like New York City, which was drawn up into blocks and separate areas and a pretty tight operation. London was more like one big mass of everything different at once, all swirling together, all chaos.

I was embarrassed by how uncurious and dull I was. It was ridiculous to live here and not even see it. I felt stupid for even asking.

Stroma was breathing on the back windows and drawing shapes. Harper asked me if we wanted to go into town with him, see a few things. We could do it tomorrow, all day if we wanted, if we had nothing better to do on the weekend. Stroma squeaked and I looked over at her, and she'd written *yEs* in one of her clouds.

We half snuck out the next morning, early. It was pretty stupid, if you think about it, asking permission to leave from someone who hardly noticed you were there. I left a note instead and we went outside as soon as we heard the engine. Harper was pulled up on the other side of the road, the curtains in the back of the van still closed, his smile the only visible thing in the grey light. He'd brought breakfast from the café where they sell that apple crumble with the peel in. Stroma was going on like she always did about it tasting like fingernails. I sounded like a grown-up, going, "Don't be rude about a present," or something, just like Dad would. I couldn't believe this stuff was coming out of my mouth.

Harper had a book called *The Fields Beneath* about how much London had spread out and filled up and changed since the days when it was a few fields and a signpost or whatever. It was on the passenger seat when I got in. He said you could see pieces of the past here wherever you looked, a past long enough to blow most New Yorkers away.

"Like that house," he said as we went past a building side-on to the main road, butted up against a pawn shop that used to be a tube station. "It's facing the wrong way because that's the way the track used to go, when that house was all by itself, a day's ride from the city, surrounded by land. There's a shot of it in the book, and a drawing."

I turned round to watch it disappearing, the house from another time that I'd never even noticed before. I thought, *He's been here five minutes and he knows more about where I live than I do.*

I was worried about what to say in the van. I can be pretty quiet in a moving vehicle. In fact usually, when it matters, I'm no good at talking. Stuff has to go through Customs before it's allowed out of my mouth. I imagine saying my thing, and I imagine the response, and the whole conversation happens, locked away in my head, with no one actually saying a word. Harper didn't have Customs. That boy asked so many questions and had so much to say, and he was just this wealth of facts and figures and crazy pieces of information. I wondered how the hell he remembered it all.

We went to Trafalgar Square and St Martin's Church and Chinatown. Places I'd seen so many times before without actually seeing them. Places I'd stared at while I was waiting for a bus, or slouched around at the back of the line on a school trip. Harper was so into everything he saw. He had Stroma on his shoulders and he was chatting with her about the buildings and the statues and the people they passed.

We went to the National Gallery. We were in there for nearly two hours. Stroma had never been before. She didn't want to leave.

I felt like I'd been going around with my eyes closed.

I got a text from Bee saying, "where r u??"

I sent one back that said, "going round the world with S and HG".

Her next one said, "Ill miss u" so I answered, "back by bedtime xx".

Harper asked me what I was laughing at and I told him. "Who's Bee again?" he said.

"My other new friend," I answered. "You'll like her."

On the way home from looking at that housing estate where the cinema is (Harper wanted to) we drove through a blossom storm near Russell Square. The street was long and grey and I didn't notice the trees until the wind picked up. Suddenly there were petals everywhere, small, pale pink and hurtling through the air. Harper had to put the windscreen wipers on to see.

Outside the flats on Hampstead Road there was a group of kids we knew, all ages. Loads of the kids from Stroma's school live there. She saw them first and hung out of the little side window, waving and shouting. I joined in and we laughed at the look on their faces, us in a souped-up ambulance, cruising past.

"The trouble with a city," Harper said, pulling into a space outside our house, "is if you leave, it doesn't miss you. You're totally dispensable. It doesn't even notice you're gone."

"That's a good thing, isn't it?" I said. "Isn't it better if things go along fine without you?"

He smiled and said he'd never thought of it like that before.

We climbed out of the van. Stroma was exhausted. It had started to rain. It didn't look like anyone was in at home, but that didn't mean anything.

"Will you be all right?" he said, and I wanted to say exactly how all right I was, thanks to him. But standing there in front of our dark sad house I couldn't make myself say much, so I just smiled and nodded.

Stroma threw herself against his legs and said she had so much news now to write at school on Monday morning. He bent right down and kissed her on the top of the head, and then he looked at me and said, "See you."

God, please, yes, I thought, and I walked up the path and put my key in the door.

We'd been in about ten minutes and Stroma was playing in her room when Dad rang. "Rowan, where have you been all day?"

I thought it was rich him putting it like that, like it

was suddenly his business. "Out and about. It's your day tomorrow, isn't it?"

He laughed in that way people laugh when something is just incomprehensible to them, like they're never going to get it. He laughed and then he said, "Mrs Hardwick phoned me at nine this morning to say she saw you getting in a bloody ambulance." His voice got louder and louder while he was saying it. I had to hold the phone away from my ear.

I said, "It's not an ambulance, Dad, not a real one. It's a friend's van."

"Did Mum know where you were? Why does that woman *never* answer a bloody phone?"

I wanted to say that Mum either slept all day because of her pills or had the TV on so loud she didn't hear the phone. I wanted to say she hadn't answered that thing in months however often it was ringing. I wanted to say she'd forgotten she even owned a mobile. I wanted to say she barely registered if we were there or not, but I didn't want him putting the words "unfit" and "mother" together, so I just said, "Yes, she knew. Did you come round?"

"No," he said. "I was working. I had meetings."

"On a Saturday?"

"So nobody's hurt then?" he said.

"No, Dad, we're fine. We were just with a friend."

"Mrs Hardwick said it was a *man*," Dad said.

"He's eighteen, Dad."

"Have I met him?"

"His name is Harper and no, you haven't."

Dad waffled a bit about how he was sure if Mum approved, he'd approve, and then I said she approved, but now I had to go and help her with the dinner.

"Can I have a word with her?" he said.

"No," I told him. "It's burning."

"Well, let Mrs Hardwick know you're all right," he said. "She'll be worrying."

Bloody Mrs Hardwick. If our life was in a book, there'd be some cosy aunt you never heard of to bustle in and cluck about and gather us up somewhere else when everything went wrong. But things didn't work out like that. There wasn't anyone else, except maybe some deads and distants and not-there-to-begin-withs. It hadn't bothered me that family was just us and not something that spread outwards like a tube map, like other people's. But I guess when there's only a few of you and the cracks start showing, you lose more than if there were thirty-five other faces you could turn to.

Mrs Hardwick was the closest thing we had to extended family and she was basically a nosy, bored old woman who smelled of talc and lived next door. None of us kids really liked her. She used to keep an eye on me and Jack for Mum years ago. She had a lot of stuff with the Queen on – cups and tea towels and plates that went on the wall. She was way too strict about what you could and couldn't touch. We always got brain-dead and grouchy at her house, and we'd end up bickering about nothing so she probably didn't like us that much either.

By the time Stroma was about born, Mrs H had given up babysitting and taken to twitching her curtains and tutting in a meaningful way.

She couldn't get her head round Mum. She thought Mum was just being rude when she didn't answer the door or didn't want a sponge cake or a nice cup of tea and a chat. After all, Mr Hardwick had died more than ten years ago and Mrs Hardwick had gone out the next day with her make-up intact and her hair neatly set and her shopping list for one, and she didn't tire of telling you either. She had no sympathy for someone who wore their pyjamas all day and left the curtains drawn and could be heard crying through the walls. I don't know; maybe she thought it showed a lack of effort.

I didn't bother to tell her we were safe and sound. She'd have seen us coming home anyway. She didn't miss a thing.

That night I didn't think about Jack, for once. I thought about Harper.

I thought about the way we'd smiled at each other for ages that morning without saying anything. I thought about how comfortable that was, because with some people, it would be weird. With some people, I'd have been yelling in my own head about how awkward it felt, but with Harper it was just saying hello without talking. I thought about how straight and white and American his teeth were; how good they were at that, whatever else you think.

I thought about the way he was too shy to shake hands the first time I met him, the way he hid his hands in his pockets and looked away.

I thought about his hands and how big he was, how tall, and how full of joy, like a kid in a grown-up's body, like the opposite of me.

I thought about how much energy he had for everything, and how fascinated he was by stuff I'd always just passed straight by.

I thought about where he'd come from and the things he'd seen and the places he'd go next. And I thought about how nice he was to Stroma, how he noticed her and talked to her and made her smile.

It was a better way than usual to fall asleep.

ten

When I woke up the next morning, the clock said 9:24. Normally, Stroma was in my room by eight, even on Sundays, but not today. Maybe yesterday had tired her out so much she'd actually overslept for once. I lay there for a bit just enjoying the fact that I wasn't needed, and then because I wasn't used to it I got up to find her.

On my way down the stairs I could hear her little voice crooning away in the kitchen, joining in with the radio. She didn't see me in the doorway. She had her back to me and she was busy. Next to her on the draining board was Mum's big flowery enamel tray with a bowl of cereal, a jug of milk and a spoon. Stroma was dipping the rim of a wine glass in a big pile of sugar on the counter. She filled the glass with juice and put that on the tray too. Then she started skewering grapes with a drinking straw, like a cocktail party kebab, and she stuck that in the glass. There was sugar everywhere, grapes all over the place, rolling off the counter and on to the floor. She put a piece of paper on the tray, folded so it could stand up. It said ROWAN.

I went quietly back up the stairs before she saw me and waited for her in my bedroom. I didn't want to ruin her surprise.

I was lying there pretending to be fast asleep when I heard the most almighty crash from downstairs; shattering glass and china and the loud, long ring of enamel, and this little panicked wail.

I took the stairs two at a time. Stroma was standing in the middle of the kitchen. Her bare feet were splashed with dark juice and white milk. The floor was covered with grapes and cornflakes and broken glass and sugar, the juice and the milk moving and curdling through them. She was standing like she was on the edge of a sheer drop, as if there was nowhere she could move to, and she was crying.

"It's all right, Stroma," I said. "Don't worry."

She said, "I tried to make things all nice and now look at this broken soup!" Her voice cracked while she was talking, sort of caved in.

I put my trainers on because they were right there by the door. I picked Stroma up and sat her on the counter next to the sink, not quite on the sugar.

She said, "Mum'll tell me off."

I said she wouldn't because she wasn't going to know, and I hoped on the quiet that Mum hadn't heard and wasn't on her way downstairs to scowl at everyone. I started picking up the big bits of china and glass and dropping them in the bin. Then I got a cloth and began mopping up the mess, squeezing the cloth out into the sink, treading on grapes and cornflakes and shards. The cloth was too slow and I kept getting fragments of glass in my fingers, so in the end I used the dustpan and brush to sweep most of it up, and then I rinsed it and put it on the boiler to dry.

While I mopped the floor, Stroma put her feet in the sink and tried to rinse them. She had a dark stain on her nightie so I took that off and rinsed it too, under the tap. She sat there in her pants, looking at me with her sad eyes while I cleared up the mess she'd made on the counter. I wiped the bottom of my trainers and put them back in the hall. Then I carried her up the stairs, which was pretty difficult because she was heavier than usual, leaning into me like a dead weight.

"Thank you for my breakfast in bed," I said while I was pulling a jumper over her head. The crown of her head showed first and then her face popped out, like she was being born out of a polo neck. She'd stopped crying by then. She was starting to look like she knew there was a funny side, even if it wasn't quite here yet.

I asked Stroma what she wanted to do. She said she wanted to go in the van again with Harper.

"We can't do that today," I said, and Stroma said, "Why not?"

"Because we did it yesterday," I said.

Stroma said she wanted to do it every day because it was fun. "But we should see Dad," she said. "So he doesn't feel left out again."

I looked at my sister and I couldn't believe how cool and resilient and generous she was. She let Dad pick and choose her, and Mum carry on going insane, and she never fought them. She never threw herself at them or made demands or bitched. Now here she was thinking about Dad's feelings and trying to take care of me.

When Stroma was dressed, we went downstairs to the sitting room. It was a quiet day. We could hear Mum walking around upstairs, but she didn't appear. Dad picked Stroma up. He wanted to take us both to the city farm and then somewhere cheap for supper. I said the city farm wasn't really my thing these days, given that I wasn't six any more.

He said, "I don't see enough of you, Ro."

I had a list in my head of things I had to do while they were out. Wash the school uniforms, clean the bathroom, make sure Mum eats something, do my history essay, cook something that isn't pasta with cheese. I shrugged and tried to look comfortable and said I was busy with schoolwork.

"And eighteen-year-olds?"

"Enough, Dad," I said. "You don't know what you're talking about."

I didn't want to be home with nobody to look after. I'd feel like a sad case, moping around like Mum, just in a different room. I called Bee, but she had stuff to hand in the next day and she'd left it to the last minute. I thought about catching up with some friends and getting loud on the high street, but actually I didn't feel like it one bit. I wasn't missing them and they certainly weren't missing me.

I wanted to see Harper.

I walked into Camden, looking for his van, but I didn't find it. I wondered what he was doing at that minute. I doubted he was thinking about me.

I went by the shop where I didn't drop the negative but left with it anyway. It was the same girl behind the counter as before. Her T-shirt said BUY ONLY WHAT YOU NEED and I couldn't agree more, but I wondered if her boss minded. She was on the phone and she smiled and sort of waved with her fingers wrapped round the wire like she couldn't put the thing down if she tried. I picked up some yogurt and broccoli and some crisps shaped like teddy bears that Stroma gets worked up over. I felt like a bit of a sad case. Two hours off and I go food shopping for my kid sister.

The girl was watching me like a hawk, like I might be a shoplifter and liven up her day. She mouthed, "Are you OK?" at me, which was clever because it could mean was I ready to pay, or did I need help, or was I actually feeling all right, without committing to anything, without even getting off the phone.

I said I was fine. She held the receiver between her jaw and her shoulder to ring up 99p and 57p and 28p on the till, and she held out her hand for the money. Then she looked at me for an extra second and muttered something like, "hang on" into the phone. She smiled that kind of smile that means you want something and then she said, "You're Harper's friend."

I said, "Yes, kind of, a bit," and the way she looked at me made me feel smaller than the stupid way it sounded.

"You met him in here? That's you?" she said and I nodded.

"How *old* are you?" she asked.

"Nearly sixteen. Why?" I said.

She laughed at me. "*Nearly.* When he told me you were a kid I thought he was joking."

I told myself she knew nothing about me. I stared her out until she blinked. I asked her name, keeping my voice light, trying not to show a thing on my face.

"Rhea."

"Funny," I said, shoving my stuff in my bag, getting ready for the door. "He never mentioned you." It made me feel good for less than five minutes.

For one thing, she was probably right. What did an eighteen-year-old from New York on some longed-out European tour need with me? All he'd done was pick up something he'd seen me drop. I'd practically stalked him since. God, it didn't mean we were going to be friends for life or anything.

I didn't see him that week. Every day he didn't show I saw a little bit more how wrong I'd been, how I'd read stuff into things, stuff that wasn't there. I didn't see Bee much either, not out of school. She said Sonny was sick so the childminder wouldn't take him and her Dad had too much work on and she had to help.

It was me and Stroma again, Stroma and me. I tried to be more enthusiastic about it, like Harper; more generous with it, like Bee. But I wasn't fooling anyone. I was pretty lonely.

I'd promised to take Stroma swimming at the weekend. I was moody and it was a horrible day and I hated the idea of getting wet and cold, but we got the bus to Archway because Stroma loved to swim. She was like a little fish. She'd go under and I'd watch the lifeguards go tense and lean forward in their seats. Then she'd bob up, somewhere else entirely, treading water with a big smile on her face, a little mermaid. You couldn't help feeling happy about how much she loved it. She loved the wave machine and the noise that meant it was starting. She loved the tube-slide that takes your skin off every metre where it's bolted together. And she loved the walk-in dryer, like a silent disco, all flashing lights and hot air that made your hair fly around.

We got the bus back with our crazy blow-dried hair and our freezing fingers and toes. Stroma was nibbling at a pack of mini digestives like a mouse. She was saying something about Neil Armstrong or capital cities, and then suddenly she was off down the street. I didn't get why until I saw the roof of the ambulance, sticking up behind a transit van, parked outside our house.

I'd told myself not to look for Harper and there he was, walking along the pavement to meet us. I looked over at our windows. Most of the curtains were closed. There was nobody watching.

Stroma was jumping up and down at his feet, and he picked her up and swung her around. She offered him a biscuit. He said thank you and pretended to eat the whole pack. He was smiling at me and I was smiling back and my face was starting to ache, but I didn't want to stop.

"What are you doing here?" I said.

"Visiting my aunt," Harper said, and I was about to say, "Really?" when I saw the look on his face.

"Very funny," I said. I felt different just from looking at him.

"Where have you *been*?" he said to Stroma in this funny way, like he'd been in agony without her. "I've been *waiting* and *waiting*."

Stroma got the giggles. It took her ages to manage the word "swimming". He asked her if she was good at swimming and then he started tickling her so she couldn't tell him because she was laughing too hard.

"She's a fish," I told him, tickling her too.

"What do you want to do?" he said. "Do you want to do something?"

I said, "Stroma will get tired out and hungry any minute. She always does when she's been swimming." I sounded like a neurotic mother when all I wanted to say was, "Yes, anything. I want to do anything. Let's go."

He said, "So shall we go get her some lunch?"

I wondered if Mum had eaten. Stroma was moving in circles chanting, "lunch yes, lunch yes," and I wanted her to stop so I could think.

Harper said, "Come on, Rowan." He pulled this sulky puppy-dog face, all bottom lip. It made me laugh. I said I'd go and check. He got back in the van while I took Stroma across the road and let us in.

Mum was in the kitchen. She was standing there, in the middle of the room, like she'd forgotten what she was doing. She sat down when we walked in. Stroma kissed her on the cheek and she frowned. I said we were going to the market and did she want anything. I took her cash card from the top shelf. I made her a cheese sandwich and put it on the table.

"Will you be all right, Mum?" I said, and she waved me away with her hands.

We came out of the house and kept walking, and I signalled Harper to meet us at the end of the road because of Mrs Hardwick.

"What was that about?" he said as I helped Stroma up into the van. She clambered over the front seats into the space at the back.

"Neighbours. What they don't know won't hurt them." I asked him what he'd been up to.

Stroma's voice piped up in the back, "She missed you!" and I turned and glowered at her. Harper laughed.

"No, I didn't," I said. "It's just you're not around, and then suddenly there you are, on the doorstep."

"Don't you like me showing up?" he said.

I tried to explain it wasn't a question of me liking it or not, it was just a question, that's all. I wondered how he spent his time. I said, "I thought you might have been somewhere good."

"I have."

"Where did you go?" Stroma asked, sounding a bit cheated.

"I went to Camber Sands," he said. "You been there?"

"No." We spoke at the same time.

"Well, this guy I met told me about it. It's only a couple of hours from here. There were people riding their horses on the beach, along the edge of the water, with the sun going down behind them. God, it was good. The place was empty apart from them and me. I slept on the beach for a night and I drove around, went to this place called the Fire Hills."

"We did miss you," Stroma said.

"Maybe we'll go there together sometime." He winked at her in his mirror.

I said I wasn't grilling him about where he'd been. It was none of my business.

"But you missed me though. Admit it."

We went to the noodle alley at the Stables. We brought a blanket from the van and wrapped it round the three of us. It was full of sand. Stroma sat in the middle, shoving vegetable ramen into her mouth with a plastic spork. I kept watching Harper over the top of her head and she must have noticed because she said, "If you want to lose me, take me to Bee's dad. I want to do cooking with Carl."

I felt like I'd been caught out.

"Don't be mad," I said. "We can't do that. I can't just call Carl up and dump you there."

"Call him, go on," Stroma said. "He said we could. He told me."

I asked her why she wanted to go. I said she didn't have to. I thought she might say something devastatingly mature about how I was always looking after her and I needed a break. I thought she might embarrass me by saying, "You're the one who fancies Harper, not me." Actually, she shrugged and said, "I like Carl. And Bee. And I want to see Sonny," which was logical enough.

When I had my mobile in my hand, I asked Harper for his number. I thought I sounded super casual, all sort of, "Oh, while it occurs to me..."

He said, "I don't have one."

"Really?" I asked. "That's a bit of a statement these days."

"Hate them," Harper said. "I hate the amount of shit they make people talk."

Stroma started giggling at the sh- word. Harper pulled a face and slapped his hand.

"They don't *make* people say anything," I said feeling defensive, thinking, *Do I do that?*

"Too much planning," he told me. "What happened to impulse? Everyone has to make ten calls first and tell everybody what they're doing and change the plan."

"So you don't have one." I was smiling now because he had such a thing about it.

"No," he said, smiling back.

"Smoke signals and surprise sightings it is then," I said. "But let me just talk shit to Bee's dad for Stroma."

Carl didn't mind me phoning. He said Bee was out somewhere and Sonny was having a sleep and he'd love to have Stroma.

I asked him if he was sure. I said I felt bad for asking.

"You've got to have a life too, right?" he said.

We dropped Stroma off in the van. She jumped out and I watched her little legs running up the stairs to the top floor, the bendy backs of her knees. I remembered Jack telling me there was no official word for that part of the body. I hadn't ever questioned if he was right.

eleven

It was different being alone with Harper. I looked at him and I knew when he was looking at me, but we never quite timed it right. It felt awkward for a minute, like we weren't supposed to be looking. We left the ambulance in Bee's street and walked down the canal, through and away from the market. The rain had started. It was tiny and fine and more just in the air than falling, like the inside of a cloud.

Harper asked me where I would be if I could be anywhere, right now. I didn't know what to say. I was very, very happy where I was, thank you.

He said how about a campsite in the South of France. "Wouldn't that be great?" he said. "Just to park up and swim in the sea and feel the sun and have bonfires at night."

He said he'd been to this one place when he was a kid, when his dad worked in Europe for a while. There were posters everywhere that said *Loup! Qui es Tu?* and everybody was keeping their dogs in at night and talking about this wolf running around the place. He said, "I saw it, in the middle of the night. I had to take a pee. The moon was full and this huge creature ran past me, black, in silhouette. I could hear it breathing. In the morning I told my folks and they didn't believe me. They said I was dreaming."

"But you weren't," I said.

He shrugged. "I don't know. I didn't think so. As soon as they said it I wasn't sure."

I told him about the French campsite we went to when I was about eleven. There were so many birds in the trees crapping on people's tents that twice a day a man walked through the place with a tape of geese squawking. "It was such a weird idea," I said. "He played it through a megaphone to scare them all off."

Harper asked me if it worked. I shook my head, remembering the man in his socks and sandals carrying around the din of geese on cassette. "No," I said. "Not really. The little birds just shat themselves even harder."

"That was the holiday Jack taught me a load of French swear words," I said. "But he told me they meant other things like 'caravan' and 'hungry'. We were both in trouble."

"*Merde*," Harper said in this funny American-French accent.

I could see that holiday so clearly. For a few days we stayed at someone's house in the mountains, an old narrow house on a steep cobbled street. It had been in their family for generations, last decorated in the 1960s, all lino and Formica. I can't remember what the place was called. I do remember *les demoiselles coiffées*, 'ladies with hairdos' – nine-metre-high needles of rock with these huge boulders balancing on the top. God knows how they got made. You could walk right up to them, at the top of a steep dry slope. I kept losing my footing on the scree and slithering down. I grazed both my knees. Jack helped me climb up. It was hot. Mum was paranoid the boulders were going to fall, even though they'd managed to stay put for thousands of years. She was carrying Stroma and she kept her hand over her head, like that would help if three tonnes of rock landed on us.

I said, "I met one of your friends the other day."

Harper looked at me, "Oh, yeah?"

I nodded. "Rhea."

"Rhea?" he said. "In the shop?"

I said, "I didn't like her."

He smiled. "She's OK. She's mostly on the phone. Like it's an addiction."

"SAY ONLY WHAT YOU NEED," I said, writing on my T-shirt with my finger. He laughed out loud. "She was mean," I said.

"To you? Why?"

"Because I'm a kid. She made fun of me."

Harper told me not to take any notice. He said, "You know way more than she does already."

"But I'm still a kid."

"Well, we all are," he said. "We are and we're not."

I asked him what that meant.

He said, "Let's play that game where you describe someone in ten words. I'll go first."

"What game?"

"Just listen. OK. You." He started counting on his fingers. "You're strong and calm. You're not vain, even though you're pretty, or silly, even though you're young, or selfish, even though you could be. That's five. You're funny and smart. You care about people. You think before you speak. You're amazing. That's at least twelve. I'd rather be around you than Rhea any day."

I said, "You forgot self-conscious, awkward, unhappy…"

"No," Harper stopped me. "You have to say thanks and smile sweetly at the end of each round. That's the rules. When you're *really* good friends, you can do the things you can't stand about each other."

I did a little curtsey, and he smiled and said, "Your turn."

It was hard. I started slowly and I didn't look at him. I remember looking at the buildings growing straight out of the water thinking, *How far can I go with this?*

"One – mysterious… Two – adventurous… Three – generous…"

"All the -ouses," Harper said. "Keep going."

"Lonely…?" And then I chickened out and counted on six fingers, "Better-at-this-game-than-me."

"That's cheating!" he said. "But thanks," and he curtseyed too.

We walked for a bit. I looked at the ground. "It's

good," I said. "It's like the speed-dating way of finding out what your friends think of you."

He said a friend of his called Jay went speed dating in New York. "He asked every single girl what their *fifth* favourite pet was. And most of them took his number, proving humour is the key."

"You're funny," I said.

"Well, good," Harper shot back. "So it's working. If I kissed you would you scream?"

"No!" I said, and I was suddenly too nervous. "I'd probably cry."

"Oh, God!" he laughed. "Is that worse?" And he didn't kiss me.

I watched him for a while, but if he looked at me, I pretended to be watching the water. "I'm not mysterious," he said. "I'm pretty straightforward."

"There's a lot about you I don't know."

"That's not mystery, that's just lack of time."

"OK."

"And I'm not lonely."

"Good for you."

"I'll take adventurous and generous. Those are things I'd like to be."

"Where are you going next on your Grand Tour?" I said.

Harper shrugged his shoulders. "I think Italy would be good. I always wanted to go to Tuscany. Oh, and Venice, but I can't take the ambulance of course."

"It must be so lovely, just waking up and deciding where to be."

"I'm lucky. I know that."

"Tell me about when you left."

He looked up at the sky. "My mum was watching behind the screen door. She didn't want me to go, but she was good about it. I got a lift into the city early, before it was light, one of my dad's friends. We were driving slow past people's houses, watching them wake up. There was a lot of roadkill on the way out of Katonah, but every dead animal I saw just looked asleep, curled up on the road, dreaming, like it was magic hour or something. There wasn't a drop of blood. I knew I'd remember that."

"Katonah?" I said.

"Yeah. It's where I'm from, a little place an hour outside of New York City. It's named after an Indian Chief. He sold the land to the White Man for some blankets and a couple of beads, way back when."

"What's it like there?" I asked.

"Green," he said. "Green and lush because of the sprinklers, and hot, except for in the woods. That's where the Indian Chief is buried. And his wife and his son who both got struck by the same bolt of lightning."

"It's one way to go."

"I grew up on a private estate in the woods. My dad was the gardener. My mum cleaned house and helped look after the horses. You should see it, Rowan. The place is full of priceless art, just lurking in the forest, balancing by the pool."

"Sounds incredible," I said.

He said, "It is. It's beautiful. It's paradise. But it's not real, you know? And it's not all there is. The town is painted all colours, everything just so. Everyone knows everyone else's stuff. And there's too much money flying around. Women drive one kid around out there in a 4x4 Hummer. Do you know what that is?"

I shook my head.

"It's a fucking tank is what it is, made all glamorous. It's a different world, Rowan." Harper looked back the way we'd come, at the cobbled downslope of the bridge, the dull light on the water.

"I wish Jack could've met you," I said.

"Why'd you say that?" he asked, and I shrugged and tried to pretend I hadn't.

"I don't know," I said. "I don't usually say that stuff out loud."

"Well, I take it as a compliment. I'm sure we'd be friends."

"I miss him," I said.

Harper was watching me and I knew he was going to ask me that question, the "How did Jack die?" question. I'd walked into it. And because he was Harper, I wanted to tell him. Maybe that's what I'd wanted all along.

Jack planned to be away for a month. Mum and Dad had helped him sort out his route – working in a couple of places, visiting people he hadn't seen for years and hardly remembered, staying on their floors. It was a big deal. It was a family project.

I remember the postcard he sent. How could I forget it? He'd been away a week or so. It was a Technicolor picture of the lake where he was staying. In a valley like a bowl, high hills all around, a thin circle of coarse orange sand. There was an island in the middle, just a mound, with a church on top. Jack said you could swim right round it if you were strong enough. It was water sport city and he loved it. He skied and windsurfed and hung out in a dinghy getting sunburned all day.

On the phone he said the lake was man-made in the seventies so people would have a reason to visit there in the summer and not just when it snowed. They flooded a whole village. The church in the middle used to be on a hilltop, looking down on the narrow streets and the school and the shops and the houses. Everyone got forced out and the water poured in.

It made me uncomfortable, the idea of a drowned town, like a place built on an old burial ground, like a house where someone has died. I imagined people still down there, floating through the streets, pale and bloated and marbled, light in their veins instead of blood. I pictured them looking up and seeing the keels of boats and the tracks of waterskis in their sky.

Of course, Jack didn't think twice about it. The lake was there and that was that. And I didn't say anything. He was leaving soon anyway, heading through into Switzerland, which he expected to look like the cover of a biscuit tin, visiting an old schoolfriend of Mum's.

And then the lake drowned him too.

It was getting dark and he wanted one more swim round the island. By the time help arrived, nobody could say exactly where he went down. He spent the whole night in that village underwater. I will never stop thinking of him down there in the dark with the moon falling on him. Pale and marbled and bloated, light in his veins instead of blood.

Me and Harper didn't look at each other while I was talking. We looked at the drinkers lounging on the towpath and the kids in canoes and the oily sheen on the water. When I was done, I listened to the drip drip from the underside of a bridge. I heard the flap of a pigeon's wings as it went past. I thought about what I'd said out loud a minute ago, about the sounds I'd just been making.

Harper didn't say anything. He took my hand and he kissed it, and then he let it go again. It was just what I'd have wanted him to do.

I didn't tell him about what had happened next. I didn't tell him about being out with my friends and my mobile ringing, and me showing off, rolling my eyes because it was only my mum, about turning the thing off. I made them laugh, throwing it into the long grass, complaining about being called. How did I know they needed me home to tell me about Jack? We were lying around in the sun, me and Jazz and Deedee and Sam, and all the girls in my year I didn't see much any more, since Jack died, since Bee and Harper. We were looking at boys and passing smart comments and talking about empty, easy stuff like music and Friday night and what everyone else was wearing.

I didn't tell him about going home, expecting nothing but a lecture about phone etiquette, and finding this quiet carnage. Mum and Dad were sitting on the sofa together. They looked like they'd been locked in a freezer overnight – clutching themselves, shivering, grey-lipped, numb. Stroma was at Mrs Hardwick's next door, probably enduring a meal of scotch eggs and aspic, but I didn't know that then. I didn't think about her.

I walked in and said, "What's wrong?" and because I could see it wasn't nothing, I half didn't want to know.

Dad patted the sofa next to him and they moved

apart to let me sit between them. I felt hemmed in and overgrown, like Alice in Wonderland. I wanted to shut my eyes and put my hands over my ears.

I didn't say it was the police who came to the house. That's how it works if someone you love dies abroad. The British consulate in wherever calls the police and they have to rush round before anyone else finds out, like the local paper or something. I wouldn't want that job – knocking on someone's door and then watching their world fall apart. You could never pay me enough money to do that.

Mum and Dad had to go out to Marseilles and meet the Foreign Office people and make funeral arrangements and fly Jack's body home. I stood at the door and waved them goodbye, while Stroma hopped around on the path like some demented rabbit with no sense of occasion. Mum said sorry, as if it was her fault Jack was dead, and she had to go and collect him and work out how to say things like "bereaved" and "cremation" and "travel arrangements" in French. Dad tried to get Mrs Hardwick to look after us while they were gone, but no one was having that – not me, not Mum and not Mrs Hardwick. So Stroma and I got left alone.

To bring someone home in a coffin you have to get permission and it costs you your savings and a big loan from the bank. The dead person you love has to be embalmed and put in a lead-lined coffin so they don't spill out all over the plane. Mum and Dad didn't tell me that. I looked it up on the Internet while they were gone.

twelve

Stroma was the kind of kid you never had to remind to say thank you. You never had to elbow her in the ribs because someone had said hello and she was still deciding whether or not she could be bothered to speak to them. If you even noticed she was there, it was a bonus for Stroma. She expected nothing. Everything she got was extra.

We took her and Sonny to the library one Friday after school, me and Bee, because Carl was smothered in paperwork and it was too wet for the park. Stroma got her first library card. It might have been the key to a magic portal, the way she was acting. She couldn't believe her luck. She was astonished we didn't have to pay. There's no way she'd expected to get all that for free.

Sonny was using the books to make towers and knock them over. I was trying to build one taller than him, but he kept smashing it and saying, "Again."

"What else is free?" Stroma said.

When I said, "School," she dropped her books on a little red table and plonked down into a white wooden chair, like her legs just wouldn't hold her. The sides of the chair were the shape of a swan. Her mouth fell open and she said, "That is *not* true."

"It is," Bee said, laughing. "The government pays for our schools; the council pays."

"For everyone?" Stroma said. She looked like one of those people on the TV who've just been told their teapot's worth more than their house.

"For everyone," we said.

You could see this warm glow travel through her, this pleasant surprise. She said, "Isn't that kind of them? What nice people." She was leaning back in her swan chair and smiling like all was suddenly right with the world. I guess she suddenly felt looked after.

That was the Friday we went back to Bee's and things started to unravel.

Carl was still smothered, upstairs in his room, and

Bee said she'd make us a smoothie and a sandwich. Stroma wanted to help. Sonny and I were kind of in the way due to lack of space, so we left them in the kitchen, stuffing bananas in the blender, buttering bread.

Sonny was into stairs. He climbed them carefully, on his hands and feet with his bum in the air. I followed him up to Bee's room. He wanted to open and shut her cupboards and make piles of her clothes on the bed. He was having a great time.

I sat down on her bed and picked up a book she'd been reading. I've no idea now what it was called, but I remember this dog-eared paperback with a monochrome cover, the colours of the bookmark sticking out of it.

A postcard. Technicolor.

I wasn't snooping. I just needed to know where it was from. I thought I was seeing things.

I heard Stroma wailing and Bee's voice in delay, and she crashed into the room before I had the book fully open. She was pale as a ghost and she said I had to come "Right now, now!" because Stroma had cut herself.

She was panicked and so was I. But not just about my sister.

Because even with the book half shut I'd seen Jack's lake with the island in the middle, the hills all around, the coarse orange sand.

I had no time to think about it. Carl came out of his room and hit the stairs the same time as me. The banana smoothie was pink with Stroma's blood. The blades had got clogged and she'd tried to free them up with her fingers. Sonny started crying because Stroma was. They were filling the house with noise.

Bee said, "I turned my back for a second. I'm so sorry."

Carl held Stroma's hand up in the air, wrapped in a reddening tea towel, and we waited for the bleeding to stop. Stroma's eyes were wide and glassy and she was screaming and she couldn't look at the towel.

"I'm so sorry," Bee said again. "I can't believe I let that happen." She was bouncing Sonny on her hip to try and make him be quiet.

Carl loosened the towel from the tiny wet mess of Stroma's fingers. Her screaming got louder. "Mmm," he said, his voice quiet and light so she'd have to stop screaming to hear him. "I think I can fix that with my magic kit."

Bee took Sonny upstairs to calm him down. Stroma

leaned against me with her hand propped up on my shoulder to slow the blood flow. She soaked up all of Carl's attention. He gave her some sticky things that work like stitches and a bandage that made her hand look like Mr Bump. He told her she was brave about thirty times and did a lot of patting her on the head. He was brilliant. Stroma's volume levels went right down. She was fine of course.

Dad phoned at about five. "Where are you?" he said. "I said I might come round and there's nobody in."

"Sorry, Dad, I forgot," I said.

"Great. Where are you?"

"At Bee's house."

"Bee? Who's that?"

"She's a friend from school. We're at her house. I'll come now."

"No," Dad said. "Don't bother. Not if you're having fun." There was this silence on the line, and then he sighed and said, "As usual I don't know where your mother is."

"Mum? She's at yoga," I said, and Bee and Carl and Stroma all looked at me. "We can be there in five minutes, Dad, it's no big deal."

I thought about getting another look at the postcard. I thought about asking Bee a few questions. I got a rush of nerves in my chest.

"I don't think so," Dad said. "Not now. It's getting late. I need to get back anyway."

"OK," I said. "Saturday then."

"Are you coming too?"

"I don't know," I said. "Maybe."

And then we ran out of things to say.

Even before he moved out Dad and I didn't do a lot of talking.

Once we had this conversation about something I'd done in history class. My teacher said that in Nazi Germany (or Cambodia or Rwanda or Bosnia), if the people who were safe had stood up for others instead of being glad they were safe and trying to blend in with the wallpaper, history would have been different. She said that doing nothing while others suffered was a crime in itself. It stuck in my head and I wanted to talk about it. But Dad just laughed and said that apathy was underrated and I had no idea how hard it was doing nothing. He said I'd learn to be more cynical when I grew up. He said that more than a million people marched against the war in Iraq and it happened anyway because ten people had already decided it would.

I said, "Who decided Jack would die and we would never get over it?"

He didn't say anything to that. He just left the room, which was Dad's answer to everything.

It's both of our faults. I should have asked him for help, and he should have known without me telling him. He should have opened his eyes, instead of pretending a couple of fun afternoons a week was enough parenting for anyone.

When we got home, Stroma watched *Doctor Who* in the sitting room and tried to get Mum to notice her hand. I went upstairs and ransacked my drawer for Jack's postcard. I pulled the whole thing out and dumped all it held on my bed, shoved half of it on to the floor while I was searching. I knew it was in there. And I knew before I found it that I was right. It was exactly the same as Bee's. I turned it over and my heart stalled a little at the sight of Jack's handwriting, black and erratic, like something crawling across the page.

SIS, THIS PLACE IS WACK.
DRY AND HOT. THE LAKE'S THE
ONLY PLACE TO KEEP COOL.
EATING FRENCH BREAD ALL
DAY, SITTING IN A PEDALO.
AND IT'S SUPPOSED TO BE
WORK! X JACK

I wanted it to be a coincidence.

I imagined turning Bee's postcard over and seeing someone else's note, someone else who'd been there and thought about home. Subject closed, mystery over. That's what I wanted.

Jack's picture was against the wall by my pillow, resting on the skirting board so you couldn't see it even if you looked under the bed. I pulled it out and stared at him. I willed him to tell me what the hell was going on. I pictured him in the room, breathing and thinking and talking and helping, not staring me out in black and white, perfect, elsewhere, full of secrets.

At first after it happened I pretended to myself that Jack was still away. He was skiing and scuba diving and climbing Machu Picchu. He was working for a relief organisation in the Sudan. He was living a wild and dangerous and knife-edge life because he had nothing left to fear.

I almost fooled myself. Sitting there on my bed, trying to get his photo to talk to me, I wished I could start pretending all over again.

When Stroma came up and started pushing on my door, I dragged myself off the bed to help her open it. I stapled a smile on my face and listened to her jabbering on about bandages and clapping games and some kid who pushed her in the queue last week and wouldn't they be sorry.

Mum was still in the sitting room with the door closed. I let Stroma in my room for a bit and then I ran her a bath. She made a big deal about keeping her bandage dry. I had to prop it up on towels. The soap was too big for her to roll it around in one hand.

I read her a quick story and stayed to listen to a couple of lullabies. Then I went back to sitting in my room, missing Jack, wondering about Bee, feeling like someone had just turned all the lights out.

thirteen

Dad and Harper met by accident.

He'd come to pick up Stroma. We'd had one of those mornings. I had to keep on at Mum to get dressed and everything was a bit tense because I needed it to look normal. Stroma was sitting on the arm of a chair, chewing a piece of toast, staring dully through the sitting-room window. She started pulling faces at me, jerking her bandaged hand around.

"What are you doing?" Dad said, and then I looked out and saw Harper, getting out of his van, crossing the road.

I stood up too fast and said, "I'm just popping out quickly."

Dad said, "Now?" like I was spoiling a priceless family moment.

I said something about the fridge being practically empty, which was true, and I got to the door maybe three seconds before Harper did. Another one and he would've been reaching out to knock. He grinned, and my stomach clenched and flipped and I grinned back. I put my finger to my lips to tell him not to speak. I could hear Stroma ferreting around in the coats and then she was in the hallway shouting, "And me! And me!"

Dad was coming out of the room behind me. He said, "Rowan you don't have to—" and then he stopped dead in his tracks and stared at Harper. "Who's this?" he said, and he sounded scared or angry or both, I couldn't tell.

I looked at Harper and for a second I saw what Dad could see – this tall, skinny, scruffy guy with a shaved head and a broken smile. I saw Trouble.

Trouble held out his hand and smiled his best smile and said, "Hello, Mr Clark. I'm Harper Greene."

Dad wasn't sure what to do. He shifted a little on his feet and cleared his throat and he didn't smile when they shook hands. Stroma and I looked at each other.

"Are you taking us to Sainsbury's?" Stroma asked,

flaunting her bandage to be sure Harper saw it, stroking it like a little mouse.

He wavered for less than an instant. "Yes, yes I am."

Dad said, "Are you the one with the van?"

"Ambulance," Harper said. The smile was still glued on his face.

Dad looked at me and back at Harper. He told Stroma she wasn't going, and she turned away from him and pulled a face, but there wasn't a lot she could do about it. He said, "We're going out now anyway, Stroma. That's why I'm here, remember?"

Then he said to Mum, "Is this friend of hers OK then? Have you met him?"

I counted to ten and I could picture Mum looking at Dad like she barely knew who he was, never mind what he was talking about. *God*, I thought. *Anything could happen.*

"I'm just helping Mum out," I called from the hallway. "She's worn out. She does everything round here."

Mum came out of the room and she looked pretty normal with her hair brushed and clean clothes on and everything. Dad was behind her. "You're a good girl, Rowan," she said. And then to my dad, "It's fine."

"Come straight back," he said. "Phone me when you do."

I could have kissed Mum. Except that would have given the game away because she wouldn't have taken it well.

Harper and I walked to the van. We drove past Stroma and Dad holding hands, on their way to the playground. Harper wound down the window and asked Stroma if she got in a fight with a shark.

"No," she said. "A smoothie."

He watched them disappear in his rear-view mirror and laughed.

"Can you believe my mum?" I said. "She hasn't said anything nice to me for months. She hasn't actually said much at all."

"Like you say," Harper smiled at me, "she's in there somewhere."

"Yep. So nice to get a glimpse."

I said he really didn't have to take me shopping and he told me not to say another word and how long would it take anyway? When we stopped in the underground car park, I handed him my postcard.

"What's this?" he said, turning it over, scanning Jack's handwriting, reading his name. He looked at me and then again at the picture.

"Bee's got one," I said quietly. "I saw it. Exactly the same."

"From Jack?" Harper said, and I said I didn't know, I hadn't seen the back of it, but what were the odds?

"Have you spoken to her?" He turned round in his chair to face me. I shook my head. "You have to ask."

"She can't have known him. That would be too weird. She'd have said something. She'd have told me."

"You'd think," he said, reading the postcard, putting it back in my bag.

Sainsbury's was too orange and shiny and loud and full. I felt like we were playing at grown-ups. I felt uncomfortable. Harper kept trying to put things in the trolley for Stroma – gingerbread people and Barbie spaghetti shapes (a handbag, a high heel, a heart, some lipstick). I snapped at him. I said I had no idea where his money came from, but I didn't have enough to give her a taste for TV tie-in junk food. I said all we had was what Dad put in the account every month and I had to make it last.

"Just kidding around," he said, holding his arms in the air like I was threatening to shoot him. He came back with some budget loo roll to make up for it and said, "I saved it, by the way. It's mine."

"What?" I said.

"My money. I worked for three straight summers dragging rocks and burning leaves and mowing lawns. Since I was fifteen. I didn't take a break and I didn't spend a cent. I earned it all."

"I'm sorry," I said. "I'm in a bad mood."

Harper said, "It's OK." He paid for Stroma's gingerbread people himself. "I've checked them." He grinned like a Cheshire cat, like a kids' TV presenter. "They're product-placement free."

Sometime that day I got three texts from Bee. A "Where R U" and a "U OK?" and a "CALL ME". I found them when I went, too early, to bed.

When I phoned, she was at Waterloo station, on her way back from somewhere with Sonny and Carl. I didn't ask where. I could hear announcements and the sounds of infinite people moving around her. I was angry with her and I didn't want to be and it was making me more angry.

"How are you?" she asked.

"Fine," I said. "You?"

"Is Stroma OK?"

I said, "Yes." Just yes.

"How was your day?"

"We need to talk," I said.

She couldn't hear me. I could tell she was walking. I pictured her in a crowd, keeping up, weaving in between and past other bodies. I had to say it again.

"Talk?" she said. "OK – when?" She didn't ask about what. I noticed that.

"Tomorrow," I told her. "As soon as possible."

"Is everything all right?" Bee asked.

"No idea," I said, and I must have sounded more like I didn't care.

We arranged to meet at the shop. The shop where Rhea worked, where it started, where I first met Harper. I couldn't sleep that night for hoping it would all come to nothing.

In the morning we were late because Stroma left this drawing behind that she wanted to give to Bee and we had to go back and get it. My saying it wasn't that important was apparently one of the seven deadly sins, which made us even later. I didn't want to take her with me. I couldn't see how this talk would amount to anything with Stroma there, but I didn't exactly have a choice. We were rushing up the hill, four of Stroma's footsteps to every two of mine.

I heard the ambulance before we could see it, the growl of its woolly engine getting closer until it drove up alongside us and Harper called out, "In a hurry?"

We stopped walking, got our breath back. I asked if he was stalking us.

He said, "God, no, I was going to Portobello. The guy over there is stalking you," and he pointed at an old man in a straw hat and made Stroma giggle. He said to me, "Have you done it yet?"

I said, "No, that's what I'm late for. You couldn't give us a lift to Regent's Park Road, could you?"

We drove slowly up the street, towards the shop. I saw Bee waiting for me outside. She was sitting at the picnic table with her back to the road, sipping something hot from a takeaway cup. Little clouds of steam rose up as she breathed.

"There she is," Stroma said, and then she yelled out the window, "Bee!"

Bee turned and waved and smiled. She said something I couldn't quite hear, pointing inside the shop, and then she picked up her cup and her bag and went in through its yellow door.

Harper had stopped to let us out. He suddenly looked pale, and kind of shaken. "Was that her?" he asked, switching off the engine. He was still looking, like she'd left a trace of herself on his retina. I got this stabbing thought that he might have noticed how beautiful she was, how much nearer his age, that he might be processing that right now.

I opened the door. "Yes," I said. "That's Bee."

"That was her," he said.

I didn't get it. "I just told you that."

"No, Rowan, listen," he said, putting his hand on my arm to stop me from getting out, pulling the door back in. He looked so serious, like he was trying to explain something important to a child. He turned to Stroma. "Jump out and straight on to the pavement, right? Climb over me."

I looked at him. "What are you doing?"

"That bag," he said when Stroma was safely out and trying to push the heavy shop door open to get to Bee. "The one she's carrying – the red bag with the girl's face on it. It's not yours, is it? You don't have one the same?"

I shook my head. "No."

"You never borrowed it?"

"No."

"OK," he said, and he had the flat of his hand against his forehead, remembering. "I was crossing the street. I saw you drop something and go inside. I picked it up."

"Yes," I said.

"Well, maybe it wasn't you." Harper said.

"What?" My voice was dry, like half of a whisper. "What are you saying?" My heart banged like I'd been running. All the glow of the morning leaked out of the day and into the ground.

"I'd forgotten about that bag," Harper said. "The person I thought was you had that bag."

"You're sure?"

He put his hand out and tucked a strand of hair behind my ear. He touched the side of my face. "I think it was Bee."

"Oh, God," I said. "She told me she was there. I didn't see her. I didn't think about it."

It was Bee who dropped Jack's picture.

Harper gave the negative back to the wrong girl.

fourteen

Bee came through the door with Stroma and the smile faded from her face because of the look on mine. Harper got out of the van and picked Stroma up by her armpits and swung her in the air.

"Hi, Bee," he said. "I'm Harper." He didn't stop moving for her to say "Hi" back. He gave me his keys and said, "I'll come and get you," and then they were gone, headed into the park, away from trouble.

There was a moment before it started, a nothing moment, when I knew I was about to ask her and change everything. I took a long time shutting the van door, locking it, putting the keys in my pocket.

"Was it you?" I said.

Bee said, "What?" but I could tell by her face she was stalling.

"Did you drop the negative?"

She didn't speak.

"Why didn't you say something in the shop if it was yours? Or at school?" She stared at me with her sad eyes. She kept her mouth shut. "You could've just said 'That was mine'," I said. "I would've given it back. I wouldn't have had to know what it was."

"Wouldn't you want to have it?" she said in this small dry voice. "Wouldn't you want to know?"

I looked at her and I tried to forget that I liked her, that I even knew her. "What were you doing with a picture of my brother?" She didn't say anything. "Will you just fucking tell me?" I said.

A lady walked past with too much make-up and a lap dog and she glared at me. I thought, *Don't say a word about my language because I will fight you.*

I let this long slow breath out. I asked Bee if the negative was hers, if she took the picture.

She said it was. She said she did.

There was this horrible silence and I tried to wait it out, but I couldn't.

"Start talking, Bee, or never talk to me again."

"I was hiding at the back of the shop, trying to blend in. I was watching you. I'd never seen you out of school before. I was just watching."

I asked her if she knew Jack.

"I knew him," she said, closing her eyes.

"How?"

"From around."

"And you hung out? You were like friends?" All she did was nod. "You knew Jack. Did you know he was my brother?"

"I did when I moved school. Someone told me."

"But you didn't say."

"No."

"And then you met me and you still didn't say."

"No."

"What, you didn't know what to say?"

"Something like that."

"So you just printed his picture in front of me and said fuck all. That's weird, Bee. That's wrong."

"I'm sorry. I was scared."

"Scared?" Bee who lectured me about fear and said it wasn't OK to go through life avoiding things you were afraid of. Bee who reckoned she'd like to die flying. I laughed. "Scared of what? Not me."

"Just scared," she said.

"Well, it's not OK. It's a shitty thing to do. I still can't believe you did it. Why would you do that to me?" I sounded spoilt. I didn't like how I sounded. But I saw her, tidying up around me while I cried, sitting like stone by the window, saying nothing.

"I did everything wrong," she said. "I didn't know what to do. I wanted to be friends. I wanted you to find out. I didn't want him to end up in the bin."

I thought about the negative, chucked in the bin in Jack's room. I only got it back out because I wanted Bee to like me.

I had this urge to move. I got up and asked her if she wanted anything from the shop, and when she said no, I went in anyway, just to get away. I looked at the stuff on the shelves and the things in the fridges and I didn't want any of them. I watched her through the window and she had her head in her hands, her hair balled up in her fists. I went back outside empty-handed and sat down.

I asked her about the postcard.

She looked at me for a little too long, so I said, "It

was in your book. I wasn't snooping. Is it from him?"

She felt around in her bag and got out the book. She gave me the card, picture side up, so I had to turn it over to find out.

Jack's handwriting was on the other. I stared at her for a beat before I read it.

GORGEOUS GIRL,
3 WEEKS AND I'LL BE HOME.
WHAT A PLACE. FAKE LAKE
WITH FAKE SAND. YOU'D
LIKE THE OLD TOWN THOUGH.
I WANT YOU TO BE HERE.
COME AND BURN YOUR FEET
ON THE ROCKS AND LIE
WITH ME IN THE SUN. MAN,
I MISS YOU. YOU TURNED
ME INTO A F***ING
ROMANTIC!
3 WEEKS BEE X X J X X

"Oh my God – you and Jack?" I said, and she nodded, her make-up running, a black line down the curve of each cheek. She wiped her face with the flats of her fingers.

I stared at the pavement. I put my forehead down on the damp wood table and looked through the gaps and I tried to think straight. Bee and Jack. Jack and Bee.

When I was born, Jack wanted more than anything else in the world for me to be a boy. We got told so many times about how he went up to the nurse on the ward and demanded she take me back. I hated that story because it left me out.

Same as when Jack and Dad watched football and got that "you're just a girl" look in their eyes. Or the time I found him and Tiger Charles trying to make a bonfire in the derelict house on Marsden Street and they wouldn't let me join in.

Jack and Bee put all of those things in the shade. They made me stand on a cliff edge of left-out-ness. My brother was in love and I didn't know it. I never noticed. He never said.

And then, when he'd gone, she didn't even come and find me. Instead she put me through this, every step, and watched me squirm.

What was the point of that?

"I can't do this," I said. "I'm not doing it."

"Rowan," Bee said. "Please listen to me."

I looked over at her. How is it possible to love someone and hate them at the same time?

"You asked me about him," I said. "You made me tell you stuff. Did you already know it all? Was it a competition?"

Her voice was so quiet compared to mine. "When we printed that picture, I thought we might talk about him. I wanted to tell you, but I got scared. You shut down. You couldn't leave quick enough."

"Yeah, well, I'd just seen a ghost."

"I didn't think you'd believe me," she said.

"Why not?"

"I don't know. I never met you. I never met any of your family. I was the last thing you needed, a stranger barging in and feeling the same way you did. It's wrong, isn't it?"

"Why didn't he bring you home and introduce you?"

"We were a secret. It was our thing."

"Did his friends know?"

"Nobody knew."

"Did you tell Carl?"

"Yes, I told Carl. Jack used to come to the house a lot. Carl knew him too." Her eyes filled up again then and she looked around her, left and right, like she wanted to run.

"Carl?" I breathed out hard, tried to think straight. I said, "How come Carl let you print the picture in front of me? How come he didn't say anything to me about Jack?"

"He wouldn't interfere. He said it was a mistake, after you'd gone, but he wouldn't have stopped it. Not his way."

I waited for her to say something else. I just looked at her.

"It's not all about you."

"Say that again?"

"It's not all about you."

"What does that mean?"

"You're not the only person who lost Jack. You're not the only one he left behind."

"You think I don't know that?"

Bee shrugged. There were whole worlds of sadness in her eyes. "I love him too, Rowan. I miss him too."

I looked over at the park, towards the sun. I could see Harper and Stroma, running in the low corner, circling with their arms out to the sides like aeroplanes, dodging each other, spinning out. Bee had that strange glow about her that you get from crying, like it's been making you sick to keep it all in. I had no idea how I felt. If someone had asked me, I wouldn't have understood what they were on about.

I got up again and she looked at me like "so go if you're going" but I didn't go anywhere. I went to her side of the table and I gave her a hug because I had no idea what to say. She hugged me back and we stayed like that for a while.

A man sat opposite us with his coffee and pretended we weren't there.

A pigeon kept coming too close to my foot.

I thought about the time I almost told Bee how much Jack would have liked her. I pictured him in that kitchen with Carl, taking the stairwells a flight at a time, standing by the front door with the geraniums and daisies.

"Were you together for long?" I said.

"About six months." Bee smiled and wiped her face again. "Six months three weeks and four days."

I breathed out through my mouth, puffed out my cheeks.

"He was going to tell you," she said. "You were the person he most wanted to tell."

"Talk to me about him," I said. "Tell me about how you met."

* * *

The first time Bee saw my brother, he was walking into Chalk Farm station and she was walking out. The wind was rushing through the doorway and his shirt was blowing flat against him and out behind. He looked like he was taking off and she laughed and so did he. And they said hello like they knew each other, even though they didn't.

She went home and thought about him. She had this picture of him in her head, walking with the wind in his shirt.

The second time she saw him was in Golders Hill Park. There was a ruined house there and even though she knew it wasn't exactly a secret, being in the middle of London and everything, she was always surprised if other people were there. She was walking towards it and she was annoyed that someone was sitting on the raised floor between the broken pillars, because that was her place. When she saw it was Jack she went and sat down, like they'd arranged to meet, like he'd been waiting. It couldn't have been easier.

The third time she saw him she said she loved him

because she didn't see the point in pretending not to and once you know you know.

"Your brother had the most beautiful skin," she said. "I couldn't stop looking at his skin. He was the funniest, sweetest, most give-everything, joy-finding, wisest human being I will ever know."

We were quiet for a while. My eyes were crying. I wasn't sobbing or anything, no dramatic stuff. Just water. I looked at the grain of the table. I picked at it with my thumb. It was soft and damp from years of rain.

I said, "You know, it's the best picture of him I ever saw."

She took it on Hampstead Heath at five in the morning. They'd just seen a man on a white horse and they were trying to work out if they'd dreamed him or not. "Jack was laughing so hard," she said. "At something he'd said, at how funny he was." She shook her head at the thought. She shook her head and stopped smiling and remembered she was sad.

"It was harsh of me to print it like that," she said. "It was hardcore. I'm never going to feel good about that."

"Forget it."

"I wanted it back. I wanted you to know. It just kind of happened. I'm sorry."

"You're right," I said. "It would have ended up in the rubbish. I didn't think it was anything. I only did it because I wanted you to like me."

"You could say the same about me," she said. "Believe it or not."

When Harper and Stroma came back, Bee got up to go. I asked her what she was doing. I said, "You know I've wanted you two to meet for ages."

"I'm going to give you some space," she said.

"You don't have to."

"I know. But I kind of need some anyway. We have to talk some more. Will you call me later?"

We hugged and it was awkward, and I told her that I'd been thinking all this time how well she and Jack would get on. Then she walked away with her incriminating bag and her sad face and her hair the same colour as mine.

Harper was behind me then. He said, "How was it?"

I did the so-so thing with my hand, the thing Stroma always called Mr Iffy. And before I could think about it or put it through Customs, I walked into him and put my forehead on his shoulder, my arms around his waist. He had his hand on the back of my head. His sweatshirt was warm. The smell of him was warm.

Stroma went, "Aaaah," but Harper didn't let go so I couldn't turn to get at her.

I said, "She knew him. She loved him."

He said, "You OK?"

"No idea. She's not. She loved him."

"Jesus." His cheek was against my hair. We looked at our reflection in the shop window.

"I wasn't very fair," I said. "I gave her a really hard time."

"You didn't fight though, right?"

"No, we didn't fight. I just made her feel worse than she did already."

"I think maybe you did that to each other. I think it's not finished yet."

I phoned Bee while we were still outside the shop and Stroma was finishing her soup and crisps for lunch. She didn't pick up. I left a message saying, "Bee, it's me. I'm so sorry. It wasn't sinking in, but it will. I love you."

Stroma was dead quiet like she knew something important was going on, even if she didn't know what it was.

Harper kept giving me these worried glances. I just wanted to be on my own. There was a big old station clock inside the shop and I kept checking the time, like every less-than-a-minute, even though I knew what it was going to say.

That afternoon Dad was supposed to be taking Stroma to Clown Town, one of those sweaty indoor playgrounds where you have to take your shoes off and everyone throws coloured ping pong balls at each other and the whole place smells like onions and feet. Stroma didn't want to go. She wanted me to phone him and try and get her out of it, but I wouldn't.

I snapped at her and she went all sulky, and Harper did this thing with his hands that meant, "Don't take it out on the kid," and I wanted to scream. I really did.

I wanted to say, "Which kid? Because I'm actually one too, remember?"

Everybody sat there without saying anything and then I stood up and said we had to go. Harper offered to drive us, but I turned him down in a cold sort of way and only threw in a thank you out of habit. There was this voice in my head, some tiny bit of me that was still calm, saying, *Don't blow it* and *What's he done?* Stuff like that, but I wasn't really listening.

My brother and Bee. That's what I was thinking, over and over, about how sad it was.

I hadn't missed Jack in a while like I was missing him right then, like a slice had been taken out of me, like a big gaping hole.

Poor Bee, missing him too.

fifteen

On the way home Stroma started asking questions about Jack. It was the weirdest thing.

She did that a lot at first, with this cold-blooded kind of curiosity, like she didn't care he was dead that much, but she just really needed to get at the facts. The whole time Mum and Dad were in France, calling every night in these leaden voices, trying not to tell me too much and then saying it all by crying just before they put the phone down. The whole time they were away and I was trying to be the big grown-up, Stroma was this seething bag of questions.

How did he die? Where did he go? Would he carry on growing? Would we see him again? Could he see us? Was he going to get burned or buried? Where?

I almost went insane.

I wasn't sleeping then either. I'm not sure how much sleep I got while we were on our own. I'd never been left before, to take care of things. I didn't even like the dark back then, for God's sake. I think I made out everything was fine, saying goodbye to Mum and Dad and all that, because what choice did we have? But that first night when the light started to go and the rooms got dark and every sound seemed strange to me somehow, too loud and kind of angry, I knew what it was going to be like.

Stroma slept of course, and ate like a horse, and walked around the house talking about colouring books just like everything was normal. I sort of hated and admired her at the same time. And I tried to answer her questions, even though my voice felt like it was coming from somewhere outside of itself, even though I thought my heart and the inside of my head must have been scooped out, just to be able to stand them.

Maybe someone else's answers would have had more icing on, but I gave it to Stroma pretty straight. I thought she deserved it. Anyway, I'm not big on icing. Mum and Dad didn't bring us up that way. I wouldn't queue up to see a weeping statue, or a woman who can heal the sick just by touching them, or the face of Jesus on a tortilla. I never believed that Jack was watching us from his new home on a cloud, or was about to be reborn somewhere else, a future midwife in India, a goatherd in the Andes.

I do believe in some miracles, earthly ones, things that happen every day and get overlooked. Miracles of probability, like the fact you get born as you and not someone else entirely.

Dad explained the maths of it to me and Jack once. "Two people choose each other out of a possible 6.5 billion and growing," he said. "They have sex countless times, and at one moment and not another of these occasions, they conceive a child." (I giggled at the sex bit, but only because Jack was elbowing me.) "For conception to happen, one out of 500 million sperm (giggle) has to get to one of 400,000 eggs (snigger), chosen at random and present in the woman's body since she was in her own mother's womb. Cell division then begins to make one unique and unrepeatable human to add to the 6.5 billion."

We were never fooled into expecting an afterlife, like the life we got given somehow wasn't enough. But it clearly hadn't stopped Stroma from checking. Maybe that's just something you have when you're little that you lose later on, a complete and total trust in the supernatural.

One of Stroma's words back then was "possible". She knew the Earth was round and gravity kept us from falling off because she'd been taught it by Mrs Hall, her teacher, and everything Mrs Hall said was Biblical Fact. But she still said the Earth and all the planets could just be crumbs in a giant's pocket – it was still "possible".

"Do you think a little bit of Jack got left behind anywhere?" Stroma asked me on the way back from the shop. My head was full with Bee and him, him and Bee.

"What do you mean?" I said.

"Well, I know he's dead and everything, and he's not coming back, because I'm not a *total* idiot," she started, "but I just thought a bit of him might be somewhere."

"Like where?"

"In his room or his pictures or that 'Sorry, Stroma' thing on my tape."

"What thing?" I said.

"My tape," Stroma said. "Didn't you hear it?" I shook my head. "Means you don't stay until I'm asleep like you say you do."

"Whatever, Stroma. What are you talking about? What's 'Sorry, Stroma'?"

"It's Jack," she said. "Little Miss Muffett is on and it's near the end of side one I think, maybe side two, and then I say, 'Jack' like this – *Jaaaack* – and my voice is really little, and he says, 'Sorry, Stroma'. And then it's Miss Muffett again and I want to know if that's an actual bit of Jack I've got, because it's his real voice and everything."

"It's possible," I said, because it was such a good thought for her to have and I was dying to hear him. I said if she played it to me, I'd show her a picture I thought had a bit of Jack in it too.

"Seen it," she said.

"No, you haven't," I said. "This isn't one of Mum's. It's a new one."

"Yes, it's under your bed and I have," she said, and then she realised she shouldn't have and made this little *um* noise, and her eyes went all wide and she looked away.

"You're not supposed to go in other people's rooms

without asking. When have you been in my room?"

"When you were in Jack's," she said, like she'd prepared that one, tested it for holes and found it watertight.

We were quiet for a minute while I swung between letting her off and getting a lock for my door. Then Stroma said, "There's definitely a bit of him in it, I think."

"In the picture you broke into my room to see?"

"Yes. It's a good one."

"Bee took it," I said and Stroma went "Huh?" and lost pace for a step or two. "You heard me. Bee took it."

"Your Bee? My Bee? That Bee?"

"Jack's Bee," I said. We sounded like one of her Dr Seuss books.

There was that "Huh?" again.

"Jack and Bee were together," I said. "Boyfriend and girlfriend."

"Like you and Harper?"

"No, not like me and Harper. We're friends. We're not anything else, not really."

"Not *yet*," Stroma said, and I thought, *God, she's too knowing for her own good, too damn precocious.* I pushed her a little, not hard, in a shut up kind of way.

"How do you know about Bee?" she said.

"I just know."

"Well, how? Did she tell you?"

"Kind of. I found out."

"How?"

"I found a postcard from Jack to Bee. I asked her."

"Where did you find it?"

"In a book in her room," I said.

"Hah!"

"Oh, OK, Stroma, the room thing doesn't matter. It's not exactly the issue here."

"What about letters?" Stroma said. "Would they be important? Would it be OK to find them in a room that isn't yours?"

"Letters?"

"Yep. Letters to Jack. I can't hardly read them though. It's all scraggly writing and scraps and some of them are *teeny*."

"Where?" I said. "In Bee's room?"

She wasn't listening. "Do you write letters to Jack? Do you think you can still read when you're dead?"

"Stroma!" I said. "You are doing my head in. What letters?"

"The ones in Jack's floorboard. Do you know about that?"

I did know. It was the place he hid his weed, the place Mum never found. He showed me once. I hadn't thought to look in it, no idea why, it just hadn't occurred. Maybe because I was the complete idiot.

"Am I in trouble?" Stroma said.

"Course not."

"Mrs Hall says there are bits of Jack *everywhere*, like dust. She said letters were a good idea and so did one of her leaflets."

"Have you told anyone else about them? Have you told Mum and Dad?"

"Duh!" Stroma said, which I took to mean she could tell them she was marrying a Martian and moving to the moon and they wouldn't hear her. She had a point.

Dad was waiting outside when we got home. He said, "Your mother is in, but she's not answering the door."

I asked if he was sure because I thought she was going out this morning, and I tried to look all wide-eyed and innocent while he studied me for signs of lying.

"I can hear the TV," he said.

Stroma said, "I left it on for the fish." She had two goldfish called Bigs and Orange that she hadn't paid the slightest bit of attention to since the day she got them. I'd almost forgotten they existed and I thought she had too.

The lie worked on Dad. I was pretty alarmed at the seamless way she handled it. He ruffled her hair and picked her up in a fireman's lift and walked her to the car. Halfway down the path he said, "Sure you won't come, Rowan?"

"No thanks. I've got homework."

He'd already turned away from me and he waved with the back of his hand while Stroma looked at me from down by his trouser pockets, upside-down and grinning.

I let myself in the house and checked where Mum was. The TV was on pretty loud, but she wasn't in there so I turned it off. I found her in the bath with the door open, steam filling up the hallway, flowering in the light.

"Dad was knocking," I said.

"Didn't hear him," she told me, turning on the hot tap with her foot.

I wondered how long this could go on before everything came apart and Dad found out, because the lies weren't going to carry on working forever.

I pulled the door shut because I didn't want Mum to see me going into Jack's room. I went straight to the floorboard, which was under his bed near the back right leg, against the wall. I crawled in on my stomach. Most of me stuck out and I had to listen for sounds of Mum getting out of the bath so she wouldn't catch me.

The broken board was about thirty centimetres long. I had to prise up one end of it with my fingernails and press down hard on the other with my elbow, and when it sprang up, it nearly caught my head between itself and the bedsprings. I felt around with my left hand and found a wedge of papers and a bag of weed I thought maybe I should give to Carl. Then I wriggled back out of there and ran down the stairs to my room before Mum was out of the water.

There were three letters from Stroma on matching paper weighed down with stickers. Everything was fairies and "make a wish…", nothing darker than lilac. Jack would have laughed at it, stuck two fingers down his throat, but now she could pretend he liked it. It was that reinventing Jack thing again, that 'make him who you like' game because where was he to argue? I wondered if I did that, which bits of him I was guilty of airbrushing.

There was a letter from me too, a really old one

apologising for something, I couldn't remember what. It surprised me that he'd kept it. I'd drawn a picture of him crying, teardrops flying out to the side like fountains and me saying SORRY in a speech bubble. I felt like it was from someone else. I didn't recognise my handwriting or the way I drew or anything. As if being eight or nine or however old I was then was like being in another life entirely. Which it was.

I didn't read mine or Stroma's letters first because I wanted to see the others. I guess I knew before I looked that they'd be from Bee. And I only looked at one, maybe one and a half, before I stopped and put them in my bag to take them back to her, because it felt like spying.

Hey J x x x
Yes yes yes let's go somewhere on Friday. I want to see those bodies in Brick Lane that are all peeled and on display. I want to see what a real heart looks like. Or we could go to mine because Carl's at work and I could look at you instead. Mmmm. Or maybe both but which one first?
   Did you read the book yet? Read it!

It's very important. What it says is you
can't live your life again and even if
you could it would be EXACTLY the
same because that's the POINT. We
are not in charge. God knows who is
(not God, you know what I mean).
    So until Friday I will wait and smile
x x x B
    Oh and Carl says I look DIFFERENT
and do I have a BOYFRIEND. I said
NO ALL BOYS ARE JERKS. So sorry
xxx He wants to meet you but don't
worry because you're going to LOVE
him. He is out there x x x x

Bee still wasn't picking up her phone, so I went
round there. I read one of Stroma's letters on the way.

Dear Jack
How are you. I am fine.
mum is stil sad and Ro is stil
Bossie.
Mrs Hall said send a ballon
but you need gas then she
said send a leter.
Ro ses your not you

enymore. rmember the time
you let me Hide under your
bed as a top seicret and no
Body found me? I do.
   Ro is beter at cooking
but not mashed pertato or
egg. wors than ever.
   I am trying to be very very
helpful.
   Bye for now. pleas right
back.
      From Stroma xxx

Carl let me in. I could tell by his face he knew what
I knew and all that, but he didn't mention it. He just
said she was in her room and kind of touched me on the
shoulder as I walked through.

Bee was reading and I asked her what the book was
and she said, "Right now it's a short story about an
Eskimo girl whose lover dies so she makes a model of
him out of whale fat."

"Then what?"

"She melts him and makes another one. I haven't
finished it yet. I'm not thinking of trying it though,"
she shrugged and laughed quietly.

She put the book down and moved over for me on the bed. I sat on the edge with my bag on my knee and I told her I found something. "What?" she said, and she shuffled back against the headboard and wrapped her arms around her legs.

I got out the pile of letters and Bee rested her cheek against her knees, held out a hand for them. I'd tied them all up with a shoelace so they didn't get lost in my bag. Her fingers were shaking while she picked at the knots. I wondered if I'd done the right thing.

"Did you read any?" she said, not looking at me.

I told her one. I said sorry.

"No, no, it's OK."

Bee spread them out in front of her on the bed. I showed her Stroma's letters too and we read one of them. It can't have been more than a couple of weeks old. She smiled and wiped her eyes at the same time.

To Jack
We did Jack and the bean stork
at story time which has got the
cow and the magic beans and the
giant who lives at the top. All the

picchers I did wer of you. This
boy max sed my clowds were very
good. The seicret is coton wool.
    If you come back then Mum
will cheer up and Dad will
come home and it will be a
good idea and more fun arond
here like befor. the only good
thing is Ro has a boyfrend who
is very nice with a van you can
live in. His name is Harper and
he is even tawler than you.
Please right soon
from Stromaxxx
    PS my best party bag is
    bulbelgum cola flaver
    a Harmonica
    A rubber that looks like money
    A key ring enything Simpsons
    Sulvanian baby twins
    Hair band or braselet or both.
    Whats yours?
    PPS bye!

173

Bee reached for this box under her bed and tipped it out on top of everything else, Jack's letters, some on torn scraps, some pages long held in their envelopes, his handwriting everywhere. "Oh, God," she said, "look at them all together," and she picked up a handful and dropped them again, like shuffling cards.

She asked me where I'd found them so I told her about the floorboard.

"I'd like to see it," she said, and I thought she meant the hole in the floor, but she was talking about Jack's room because she'd never been.

I said she could come right now, any time, whatever she wanted, but she said, "Not today. I'm going to look at these today, put them in order." And she ran her hands over them all lying there on her bed. She was smiling.

I thought maybe I should go and I said so, but she didn't really hear me. "Do you want to be alone?" I asked her.

Bee didn't look up. She just nodded and said, "Do you mind?"

I left the room and shut the door.

"Thanks Rowan," she said from the other side.

* * *

Carl was sitting in the kitchen and he got up when I went past. I gave him the bag of weed. I said, "It was Jack's."

He said, "Do you want a cup of tea?" and I didn't really, but I stayed for one because of the way he asked me, like I'd be doing him a favour.

He didn't say anything while he was making it. Sonny was opening and closing the fridge, over and over again, talking to himself. I felt a bit awkward sitting at the table looking at my hands. When he put the mug down in front of me, I sipped at it, even though it was too hot, because I had nothing else to do.

"She told you then," he said, and I nodded. I'd burned my tongue on the tea and there was this numb fuzzy patch at the tip of it. "I'm glad you know. I'm sorry we took our time about it. Are you OK?"

"Me?" I said. "Yeah, I'm fine. I had no idea, but it's fine."

Carl let out a big long sigh. He rubbed his hands in his hair like he was washing it. He picked up Jack's bag of weed and put it down again. He smiled this tight-lipped, unhappy smile.

"He was a great kid," he said. "Part of the family." I said I was glad about that. "You and Bee have been so alike," he said, "with your brave faces, getting on with it."

175

I thought about Mum. I wished she would get up in the morning and get dressed. I wished she would smile and speak and get on with her day like the rest of us. I started telling Carl about the black hole Mum was in and how if I thought about it too hard I could feel it coming to get me too, like putting your hand over the nozzle of a Hoover. I was saying this stuff and only really looking at it after it was out.

"I don't have time to fall apart," I said, and Carl laughed, but it wasn't meant to be funny.

"You're a great help to her, I know that," he told me, and I wasn't sure if he meant Mum or Bee or Stroma. "Come back soon," he said when I got up to go. "You still have a lot to talk about."

sixteen

My phone rang just after I left. I didn't know the number and I almost didn't answer.

It was Harper. "Because of you I had to get a cell phone."

"Why?" I said, smiling.

"Because I need to call you and so I have to stop at a callbox and then I don't have change and… I thought, enough. So now I have one and this is my number and there is to be no talking shit, do you read me?"

"Roger Roger, Over and Out," I laughed. "See? What did you need to say?"

"I was checking up on you. You were sad today. And rude."

"I'm sorry."

"Don't mention it. Totally understandable. Where are you?"

"Leaving Bee's."

"How is she?"

"No idea. I just gave her back her love letters."

"Do you want to meet me?"

"Yes."

"Good. Can you get to that bookshop on Harmood Street? I could catch up with you around there."

The light was greying. Not dark yet, but things were losing their edges. I know that walk so well I can do it without thinking. My brain switches off and goes somewhere else, like when you're writing something down at school and you stop hearing the teacher's voice, but your hand keeps writing it anyway. I was miles away and I nearly walked straight into him.

"Where's the limo?" I said.

"Parked up. I've been walking. How are you?"

"Fine."

We started back the way I'd come.

"Let's try that again," he said. "How are you?"

"I keep thinking about Bee," I said. "She's eighteen and she's already lost the person she loves. What could be worse than that?" I thought, *Never meeting him, maybe,* but I didn't say any more.

I told Harper about the pile of letters on Bee's bed, about how it must feel to have only those left. Letters and photos instead of flesh and blood. I said, "You should see Stroma's."

"Stroma's what?"

"Letters to Jack. I had no idea she thought about him. Not that much."

"Of course she does. He's her brother."

"She thinks there's a postbox to the other side in his room. I seriously think she's expecting a reply."

"That kid is something else. Maybe we should send her one."

"You know, I have to go home," I said. "Stroma'll be back soon. I can't deal with Mum and Dad in the same house. I need to be there so he'll leave."

"Why are you doing all this yourself?" he said, and I asked him who else there was to do it. "I don't get why you don't tell your dad."

"Because I don't want to live with him. I don't want Mum to wake up one day and find she's lost all her children."

When we got to the house, Dad and Stroma weren't

back yet and I didn't want Harper to go. "Do you want to come in?" I said.

"Not sure I'm welcome, are you?"

"You are with me."

I checked on Mum in the sitting room. She was asleep on the sofa, curled up with a blanket over her. Her sleeping pills and a glass of water were on the table by her head. I sneaked in and counted how many were left, out of habit.

We went upstairs. "Do you want the grand tour?" I said, trying to lessen the embarrassment I felt at taking him into my tiny, stupid room. I pushed the door, expecting him just to look and keep moving, but he went in and sat on the bed.

"It's like the ambulance," he said.

"Pretty compact, you mean."

"Perfect. I like it. And you'd be all right in mine. You'd be used to it already."

"Where shall we go?" I said, half joking.

"Anywhere you want," he joked back. "Just name the day."

I asked him if he wanted to see the photo, the picture of Jack he'd given me before I met him. I reached down and felt for it and handed it over. Harper looked at Jack for a long time and Jack stared right back. It was the closest they'd ever get to being introduced.

"That's my brother," I said, breaking the silence with the obvious.

"Pleased to meet you, Jack."

I thought of Bee standing there with her camera, of Jack laughing and being high and so into her. "He was with Bee," I said.

"And look how happy he was."

I took Harper to Jack's room. I hadn't done that before with anyone. He was respectful up there, hushed and careful, like someone was sleeping. I said Jack would've preferred it if we'd jumped on the bed and cranked up the music, but I appreciated it, Harper's sense of occasion. He was quiet and he put things back in the right place, and he took it all in.

He loved Jack's 'Map of the Universe'. He studied it and shook his head and laughed out loud at how microscopic and insignificant we are, almost exactly like Jack had done the first time he saw it.

I said, "I'll give it to you one day. I'd like you to have it."

"You don't have to do that," he said.

"I know that. But some day this room is going to have to be dismantled so…" I got this picture in my head of me in my thirties, with a job and a mortgage and all that, Stroma grown up and Jack still sixteen, with his room untouched and his photos faded. It was so wrong. A wave of how wrong it was hit my chest. I wasn't supposed to get older than him.

Harper picked up Jack's guitar and pulled a face that said, "Is this OK?" I nodded and he started tuning it, holding his head close to hear, bending the notes in and out.

"You play guitar?" I said.

Harper said, "A little," and then he started playing this thing that was so sweet and sad and simple, like a circle of music the way it kept going, and I said, "Liar."

I didn't hear the footsteps because I was listening to him play. I was the happiest I'd been in a while just sitting there and listening. I didn't see the door opening because I had my back to it and I was watching his hands move. I only turned round when Harper stopped.

Mum was standing in the hall, staring at him. There was so much in her face where normally there was just a blank.

I said, "You OK, Mum?" She didn't say anything.

She turned away like a slow ghost. I heard her go and lie down on her bed next door, could hear the creak of the mattress and the awful silence.

Harper said when she pushed the door open she looked like she'd just won a prize. He saw the disappointment bloom on her face and she didn't move. "She just stared."

I thought about Mum waking up all groggy in the dark downstairs and hearing footsteps in Jack's room. Not just footsteps; boys' footsteps and a boy's voice, a seventeen-year-old's, a guitar playing more than six stilted notes.

It must have been like waking from a bad dream. She must have thought her boy was home.

Harper said he should go and I didn't argue. We walked past Mum's room on quiet feet, our movements exaggerated, the closing of a door, each tread on the stairs, slow and soundless.

"What are you doing tomorrow?" he said while I was trying to open the front door without clunking. We were whispering. "Will you be all right?"

"Course," I said, but how did I know? Probably not.

"I'm sorry, Rowan," he said. "That was bad."

"It's not your fault," I said. "It's OK."

He kissed me on the cheek, so warm and quick, and his hand was on my neck, and then he walked down the path into the street. I couldn't see the ambulance, but I stood in the open door listening to it cough and start up and drive away.

I went up to see Mum. She was lying on her back with her arms above her head. I sat on the bed, gently so it wouldn't annoy her, so she wouldn't feel crowded. I said, "Sorry we scared you."

Her eyes were sort of glistening in the half dark and I could see she was looking at me. I carried on. "He's my friend, Mum. You'd like him."

She breathed out and turned her head away from me. I stayed there, not knowing what to do, getting ignored until I heard the key in the lock and Stroma's bright voice in the hall.

I knew nothing I could do would help. She'd lie there till the morning and probably even after that, and it would be my all fault.

Stroma's cheeks were bright red from all the indoor

running and Dad was smiling. They must have had a good time.

I should have told him about Mum there and then. I should have told him what just happened and what had been going on for weeks. But I didn't want to watch his smile disappear. I thought that would do more harm than good. Another great decision.

Stroma was tired out and Dad stayed for a while and made us some pasta. Part of me wanted Mum to come down and give the game away in some spectacular fashion – let Dad find out without me doing the telling. I had to force myself to sit down. I kept jumping up to rinse pans and wipe surfaces, and I was feeling a bit speeded up, a bit quicker than everything around me.

It was good though, to eat something I hadn't cooked. I caught myself pretending Dad hadn't moved out at all; that this happened every night and I wasn't responsible for absolutely bloody everything after all.

"How's Mum?" Dad said. Stroma and I stopped chewing and stared at him.

"Not so good," I said. I was thinking, *Just tell him, just ask him for help. It won't kill you.*

"In what way?"

"She's got the flu," Stroma said. "She's in bed sleeping." I looked at Stroma and she stuck her chin out and glared back.

"What? How long's she been sick?" Dad said.

I wanted to say, "Oh, years, didn't you notice?" but Stroma said, "Since yesterday," before I could think it through. That girl was frighteningly good at lying.

"Have you been managing all right?" he said and I wanted to hit him. I really did.

I looked at my food and Stroma said, "It's OK, Dad. We're good helpers."

"Does she need anything?" he said, getting up. "I'll go and see her."

"No," I said a bit too quick. "It's fine, Dad. I've just been up there. She's sleeping."

There was this awful count to five while he decided whether to sit down again or not. I could feel Stroma holding her breath beside me. Then he said should he stay the night, he could sleep on the sofa, and on and on, until I said, "Dad, I'm fifteen years old. You can go home. It's fine."

We practically had to push him out the door.

As soon as he left I said, "Why did you lie to Dad?"

"You do," she said. "All the time."

"Well, I wasn't going to tonight. I was going to tell him. Mum's really bad, Stroma. I think we need his help. I don't want to lie any more."

"If Dad thinks Mum is sick, he won't love her any more and he won't come home so we're NOT telling on her," Stroma said. Her face started to cave in and her shoulders started to heave up and down, but she kept it together and she didn't cry.

"What if she gets worse and not better?" I said.

"Don't say that."

"We have to think about it, Stro. Maybe we're not such good helpers after all." I tried to give her a hug, but she was all angry and turned away. I know that feeling anyway, when if someone comforts you or is a bit too kind, you're just going to fall apart all over the place and make a big mess.

Me and Stroma couldn't do this any more.

I dug out an old family video when Stroma and Mum were both asleep and I was all by myself for once with a TV.

Jack used to have this thing about Princess Diana, about how if nobody had told us she died, we could all have survived on TV clips alone, getting out of cars, attending galas, stroking children. There must have been tonnes of stuff on film that no one had seen yet, enough to last for years. He said that seeing as most of us never actually clapped eyes on her for real, how would we know the difference?

Watching us all in the past, unthinkingly, carelessly happy, I wished I could say the same about our family. I wished I had enough unseen footage to pretend things were the same as before.

The first bit of film was of me and Jack in a paddling pool; pretty young, sunhats and pants, the usual stuff. We were splashing each other and laughing and pouring water on our heads, and Mum and Dad were laughing behind the camera, you could hear them. Then I started wailing about something – a watering can in the eye maybe – and Mum came into view, all smiles and big shades and long hair. She was so pretty and she was wearing this thin dress and nothing on her feet. It just froze me to the sofa seeing how young and lovely she was then.

I fast-forwarded it for a while, stopped to look at me as the grumpiest bridesmaid on earth, Stroma walking and falling over balls in the garden, Jack waving from the top of a tree, endless football, several birthdays. I was thinking I should show Stroma the tape, remind her of the way things started. Then this line of crackle went down the screen and there was Jack like I remembered him, headphones on, shining and full of it, singing into the camera, filming himself. He was so close up he could have been in the room. Once he stopped singing, the crackly line came down again and it was back to some party we'd forgotten we had – Dad at the barbecue, Mrs Hardwick and her husband, Mum laughing.

Jack had basically crashed the family album, hijacked it. And I just played him and rewound him, played him and rewound him, played him and rewound him, until my eyes were so tired I couldn't see him any more.

seventeen

The next day started out like all the rest. I turned off the alarm and sleepwalked to the kitchen to make Stroma's lunch and have a cup of tea. We had an argument about Ready-Brek because she asked for it and then wouldn't eat it, and then I started stressing out about being late (again). I had to give her a piggyback to the bus stop because she refused to run. She was getting good at that, digging her heels in and winning. Mum was still in bed when we left. We crept in to say goodbye to her and crept out again. A pretty ordinary morning really, nothing to write home about.

After that, a lecture about my time-keeping, double English, an apple because I hadn't actually eaten any breakfast (too busy arguing about Stroma's), double biology and then lunch, when I went to find Bee.

She wasn't there. I called her.

"I couldn't face it," she said. "I didn't sleep so well. And Sonny's childminder was sick so I stayed home with him."

I asked her if she needed anything. If I could bring anything round.

"I need to talk to you some more. Just you and me, no Stroma. I hope you don't mind."

"Of course not. I'll sort something out."

After school I called Harper. He said his phone ringing made him jump. He said it sounded like giant crickets. He had me laughing straightaway.

"I'm sorry about yesterday," I said.

"Forget it. Me too. How's your mum?"

"Asleep, last time I looked."

"I had a good time," he said. "It meant a lot, you showing me Jack's room and everything, so thank you."

"You know Bee's never seen it."

He made this noise, this out-breath that meant "poor Bee". "I'd like to meet her," he said. "I don't know her."

"There's time for that." I said she wasn't at school.

I said she needed to talk some more. I said would he look after Stroma maybe?

"I can do it tomorrow. Is that OK?"

I was at Stroma's school gates. I could see her lining up in the playground, talking non stop to Mrs Hall. She waved at me, jumped up and down.

"Got to go. Tomorrow is perfect. Thanks, Harper."

"Bye, beautiful," he said.

As we turned into our street I saw Harper's ambulance outside the house and I thought, *He couldn't wait to see me*, and I speeded up. But I can't have seen it right because then the ambulance put its lights and siren on, pulled away and hammered past us. Stroma put her hands over her ears.

Dad's car was there. Mrs Hardwick was standing at our front door, like a policeman at No 10 Downing Street, only dressed in tweed and white as a sheet. I asked her what was going on.

"You can't go in," she said.

Stroma put her hand into mine. "What's happened?" I said.

Mrs Hardwick just shook her head. "You can't go in. You've got to come to my house."

"Where's my mum?" I said.

Mrs Hardwick's eyes followed the path of the ambulance. "Your dad's with her," she said. "And he told me not to let you in."

I crouched down in front of Stroma. She was starting to snivel. I held both her arms and I looked into her eyes and I said, "Go with Mrs H. I'll be right there. Please, Stroma. It's OK."

Mrs Hardwick was still standing there like all five foot two of her could stop me getting into my own house. She said, "You really shouldn't. It's for your own good."

I felt very calm right in the middle, like the eye of a storm. My hands were shaking. I said, "No offence, but I've been running this family for a while now and I think I'm old enough to look after myself."

She didn't argue and I was glad she didn't try. I got the keys out of my bag and I waited for her to move out of the way. I opened the door and closed it behind me and leaned my back against it, just breathing. I could hear them retreating down the path, Mrs Hardwick's voice oddly gentle, and Stroma's little sniffing noises.

Mum.

I dumped my bag and I walked across the hallway and into the kitchen. My steps sounded louder than they should on the slate floor. Everything was tidy and clean, just like I left it. She must have had a cup of tea. There was a mug on the side, rinsed, upside-down. It left a ring when I picked it up.

The sitting room was tidy too. She'd folded her blankets and made a neat pile on the sofa. Usually it was me who did that. The TV was off and the fish were there watching me. I left the room and took the stairs three at a time to my landing.

There was a note on my bed in an envelope, in Mum's handwriting. That's when time doubled up on itself and I really started moving. Mum didn't write letters. Mum didn't have anything to say.

I left it where it was and this strange noise came from the back of my mouth that I didn't even connect with me for a second, until I realised I was making it and I sounded really scared.

I can't remember taking the next set of stairs. I burst

into her room. The bed was made. There was no dirty laundry on the floor. It wasn't normal.

The bathroom was where she did it.

I should have noticed the blood on the stairs, but I didn't see it till later.

The bathroom looked like Bee's bathroom the day we printed Jack's picture, the day she fitted that red light bulb and the whole place drowned in one colour.

The bathroom was red.

The bath was full of red water. Red had run down the sides and on to the mat on the floor. Red made patterns on the square white tiles, on the shower curtain. I didn't think a body could hold that much blood.

I had blood on my hands, but I didn't remember touching anything. The door handle was bloody. Everywhere was wet with cooled steam and blood, and there was this smell, like the butcher's, like metal, like earth.

I don't know what I did next. It's like things just went blank because when I got to Mrs Hardwick's, time had passed differently for them. Stroma was eating toast on the best rug and watching the TV. She didn't see me. Mrs Hardwick hugged me when she opened the door. I remember how soft and powdery her skin felt, and the strange sweetness of her perfume.

"Where is she?" I said.

"UCH."

"Can you keep Stroma?"

She nodded and put twenty quid in my hand. "Get a taxi, dear," she said.

I had blood on my face. I looked at my reflection in the cab window. I must have wiped my eyes and got it on myself. I looked like a warrior. I tried to get it off, but I just smeared it in with my snot and my tears and the blood on my hands. The cab driver kept looking at me in his mirror and I was thinking, *Don't talk to me don't look at me don't ask me a thing.*

I got out and gave him the twenty quid and I didn't wait for my change. Then time slowed down again when I hit reception. The woman at the desk took what felt like three hours to look up at me.

I said, "Where's Jane Clark? I'm looking for my mum." And she took another three hours looking at the computer and fiddling around. I couldn't slow my breathing down.

Then Dad came out through some double doors and he had red on his hands and red on his shirt and he was trying to wipe his hands on this used up piece of tissue and he was crying.

I thought, *Please don't let her be dead. Please, God, don't let her be dead.* And I started to shake like there was an earthquake in there, but it was only underneath me.

eighteen

I've thought about it since, how come Dad didn't know about Mum, how come I didn't tell him. Of course I have. And I feel bad about it. I really do.

I've thought about why I tried to deal with it all myself and just messed up everything, how I managed to turn real life into broken soup instead of just breakfast.

I must have had my reasons, but I'm not going to try and name them.

Who knows? Sometimes you open your eyes and realise you've been going through life with them closed. And what you thought was the world was just the inside of your head all along.

Mum wasn't dead. Not for lack of trying.

She wasn't dead because of Dad letting himself in the back door when nobody answered, walking round the house, ending up in the bathroom.

"I nearly didn't go up there," he said. "I thought everyone was out."

"Why did you go round?"

"I wanted to see you. I left work early. I wanted to be there when you got home from school," he said.

"She left a note on my bed."

He said, "What if I hadn't gone upstairs?"

He said, "Where did my life go – breaking in to my own house, finding the person I love like that in the bath?"

He had my hand in his and we stayed in the hallway, drinking rank, scalding coffee, blinking under the strip-lights like lab rats.

"I'm sorry, Rowan," he said, and he was studying my hand like he'd never really looked at it before. He smiled and he was so hollowed out and unhappy, and I smiled back, but I bet I looked the same.

"Yeah," I said. "Me too."

* * *

About eight o'clock my phone rang. I took it because it was Bee. I had to go outside because phones weren't allowed in the building and people were giving me stick for it just by looking.

There was a strange half world outside the hospital. Patients were wandering around in their backless gowns, drinking coffee at silver tables across the street, standing at cashpoints, smoking with their pyjamas on. Like ghosts in the real world, like extras on a film set.

"Hey," Bee said. "Where are you?"

"I can't talk really."

"Why, what's up?"

"I'm at UCH," I said. "My mum's in the hospital."

I could hear her breathe in. "What's happened?"

"She cut herself," I said, and I started to cry again. People were looking.

I said would she do me a favour. I said Stroma was at Mrs Hardwick's and she didn't know her very well, and she didn't know anything really, only that Mum was in an ambulance. I said, "She's there on her own and she's going to be scared. Will you get her? Can she stay with you and Carl?" I couldn't speak properly because my voice wouldn't stay in one place.

"Of course she can," Bee said. "I'll go right now. We'll pick her up in the car. Give me the number."

I did and I asked her not to tell Stroma anything. "Just say Mum's fine."

"Is she?"

"I don't know."

Bee asked if it was an accident and I didn't say anything. "Oh, God. Oh, Rowan." She was all muffled like she had her hand over her mouth. I wanted to stop talking now.

"Let me know when you've got Stroma," I said. "I want to make sure she's all right."

"What about you?"

"What about me?"

"Who's looking after you?" she said.

"My dad's here," I told her. "And anyway, I'm sleepwalking. I'm not awake."

I stayed there for a minute, looking at the rain falling out of the dark in the orange lamplight, and the lamplight in the puddles, and the endless rhythm of people getting on and off buses, crossing roads in the traffic, like a pulse. And then I turned and went back into the hard glare and the swing doors and the shiny floors and the waiting.

I must have slept where I sat because the nurse woke me up, talking to Dad. She was saying things about "immediate risk" and "possible nerve damage". She said Mum was sedated and that the psychiatric people would be assessing her as soon as they could.

I said, "Do you want to know what drugs she's on?" The nurse looked at me with this tight smile. "For sleeping and stuff. I've got a list with the dosage and everything."

The nurse said someone would come and get that information from me later. Her smile didn't budge, and she and Dad both carried on looking at me for a second too long. I closed my eyes and pretended not to be there until she'd gone. Her shoes made a squeaking sound on the floor, really loud and high-pitched. White lace-ups. I couldn't have worn them.

Nobody came of course. I gave the list to Dad and he read it for a while, then put it in his wallet. He said, "Why didn't you tell me, Rowan?"

I didn't answer. I kept my eyes shut and I didn't speak.

Bee texted me to say that Stroma was fine. She said, "Call me if u want or need" but I didn't know what to say so I didn't.

I told Dad that Stroma was at Bee's. I told him she'd be happier there so he didn't have to worry. For a second he almost looked like he'd forgotten who Stroma was.

He said, "You should go home and get some sleep," but I didn't want to be alone with the bathroom, and when I said so, he went pale and he put his head in his hands and breathed out hard, like a horse.

"It was hard, carrying her out," he said, and he was looking straight at the memory of doing it. I figured it was him that got blood on the floor and the walls and the door and the stairs. I imagined Mum just bleeding quietly into the water.

We slept in our chairs, on and off. There was a draught and it was noisy, and everyone we saw had this shocked look about them, like this wasn't the day they'd been expecting by a long way.

Jack and I used to play the *Casualty* game. You had to watch the first five minutes of the programme while they set up the stories – lonely old lady with six cats and a rusty tin-opener; victim of a bully finding a gun in a dustbin – and then you had to predict who was heading for the ambulance, and how, and if they'd see out the day. *Casualty* itself was pretty rubbish so we'd turn the sound down and play cards and wait to see who was right.

I didn't see any old ladies with tetanus or any gunshot wounds. Mainly I saw the wall in front of me, a sickly sea-foam green with pock marks and little pin holes, like the back of Jack's door where he used to keep his dartboard.

In the morning Harper came.

I thought I was dreaming. I got up and my body was stiff and kinked out from living in a plastic chair. I said, "What are you doing here?" and then I held on to him and I wouldn't let go.

His voice in my ear said, "Sssh," just quietly, over and over, like listening to a seashell. He smelled of cut grass.

I said, "How did you know?" and he said, "Bee."

He told me she came on her bike, rode around looking for him, banged on the window to wake him up.

Bee did that for me.

Harper took his jacket off and I put it on. It was only then I realised how cold I was. He asked me if I needed anything, something to eat, a drink of water.

"A time machine maybe," I said.

He asked me if I found her.

"No, my dad did. I just went in after."

"I'm sorry," he said.

Dad was watching us from where he was sitting. Watching us and staring straight through us at the same time.

"I was doing everything I could. I was helping."

"It wasn't you, Rowan. There's nothing you could have done."

"Do you think it was us in Jack's room? Do you think it was that?"

"It's grief," he said. "It's chemicals in the brain. It wasn't us and it wasn't you."

A nurse was talking to Dad. I went over and she said it all again, like a waitress doing the specials. Mum was awake, but heavily sedated. We could go in, but one at a time, and only for a few minutes. She was very drained.

Dad went in first. He squeezed my hand like he was wishing himself luck.

I went back to where Harper was standing. I said, "What's it like outside? What kind of day is it going to be?"

"It's a good one," he said. "Come and see."

You couldn't see the sky from where we'd been all night. You couldn't see outside at all. I don't know if that was to protect the healthy from the sick, or to stop the sick seeing what they were missing.

Harper was right. It was a good morning. Big blue-violet sky, last night's rain shining on the road, the gaps between the buildings day-bright and peppered with cranes. People moved past us double time, oblivious, on the phone, scanning the paper, sipping on coffee, one last smoke before work. Business as usual except for those of us who couldn't remember what day it was. I wondered if I should phone school or if that was Dad's job now, if they'd even believe me.

"Do you think things will start to get better now?" I asked Harper, as if he knew.

He was squinting into the sun and said, "Well, I suppose they could have been worse."

After a while, Dad came out to join us. He looked so strange in the outside light, with his bloodstained shirt and his tear-stained face, like an actor playing my dad, like the person I didn't know underneath.

He said, "Go in and see her if you want to. You don't have to."

I left them there together, Dad and Harper. I was too busy controlling my breathing to wonder what they'd find to talk about.

Mum was lying on her back with her hands palm up at her sides. Tears fell the shortest way from her eyes to the pillow, straight down, making little pools in her ears. I bent down and she put her arms around my neck and I kissed her cheek and I shook from not crying.

I said, "Don't do that again, Mum." She closed her eyes and let her arms fall back on the bed.

I said I was sorry if I'd done the wrong thing and she shook her head, and the tears moved faster to the pillow, like rain on the car window when you're driving through it. She didn't ask about Stroma, but I told her anyway. I said she was being looked after. I said, "She doesn't know."

After that I didn't know what to say, so I kissed her again and I smoothed her hair with my fingers. It was odd being able to touch her. She didn't pull away while I did it. She didn't look at me.

Afterwards I said to Dad that I didn't think Stroma should see her. Not yet. He said one of us should go and tell Stroma that everything was OK, and could that be me because he wasn't ready to go yet, he wanted to stay here with Mum.

Harper said he'd take me to Bee's. I wanted to stop by the house and pick up a few things for Mum, like her toothbrush and some pyjamas, maybe a long-sleeved cardigan or a dressing gown. I thought it might help. I kept talking about it in the hospital car park.

"How much sleep have you had?" Harper asked me.

I didn't know. "Not much."

He made me a bed in the back of the van. He folded the sofa down and got out the bedding. I was too tired to argue. The sheets smelled of him. I wrote him a list of what I'd thought Mum needed and I gave him my key. I fell asleep with the purring of the road beneath me.

Stroma got under the covers and woke me. She lay on her side in front of me and put my arm round her waist, shifting to make the same shape with herself as I had, to fit exactly. I snuggled in a bit towards her, opened my eyes.

"How's Mum?" she said, like she knew without even looking I was awake.

"She's sleeping," I said.

"What happened?"

"She hurt herself in the bathroom."

"How?"

"I don't know. Maybe she fell."

Stroma giggled. "Silly."

"Yep," I said. "Silly."

Harper pulled out into the traffic and me and Stroma rolled a little in the bed.

"I like Carl," Stroma said. I nodded into her hair. "We did flower pressing. Guess what Bee showed me," she said, turning to lie on her back, all elbows and knees. "Pictures of Jack. Loads and loads of pictures of Jack."

"How lovely," I said.

"Can I tell Mum about Bee being Jack's girlfriend?"

"No," I said. "Don't talk about Jack with Mum, not today."

"Why not?"

"She's too tired, Stroma. You don't get much sleep in a hospital."

"Why? You need sleep when you're sick. That's what Mrs H said. She said Mum would be having a nice long sleep. You said she was asleep."

"Just don't talk about Jack, Stroma. It makes her sad."

"*Everything* makes Mum sad," Stroma said, and she moved away from me slightly, kept her eyes on the roof of the van.

I asked Harper if he got Mum's stuff and he pointed at a carrier bag on the seat next to him. I sat up and looked at the clock on the dashboard. It was after twelve. "What took us so long?" I said.

Harper looked at me in his mirror. "I had a little clean up."

I didn't get it for a minute.

"I went to get her toothbrush," he said. "I couldn't leave things like that."

"Like what?" Stroma asked, while I tried to tell Harper how I felt just by looking.

"Your mum made some splashes when she fell," Harper said. "The bathroom was a bit wet."

I got out of the bed and I put my arms around his shoulders from behind. Harper rested his head against mine. "I can't believe you did that,"' I said quietly.

Stroma was going, "Did what? Did what?"

Neither of us answered.

nineteen

Stroma went straight to the bathroom when we got home. As soon as the door was open she started up there, hit the stairs running like she wanted to make sure we weren't hiding something. She missed the bin bags Harper had put outside, full of towels and cloths and water and Mum's blood. I followed her up there slowly while he looked in the fridge for something to eat. I didn't want to go in, even though I knew there'd be nothing to find.

I was standing outside Stroma's room. She was on the loo. I listened to her washing her hands and I heard her walk towards the door, and then I glanced back and saw the envelope on her bed. White like the one on mine, and when I got closer I could see it was Mum's writing. I kind of went white hot, and when I picked it up I wasn't entirely sure my hand would work and I bent it in half and shoved it in my back pocket when Stroma walked in.

"What?" she said.

"Nothing."

"What have you got?"

"Nothing, Stroma," I said, and I started to walk across the room.

She stamped her foot and screwed up her face at me. "What have you taken from in here?"

"I haven't taken anything."

"Liar! Give it back."

I pushed past her and I said it again. "I haven't taken anything," and I started going downstairs.

"Right then, well, I'll take something from yours," she said, and she tried to pass me on the stairs.

Mum's letter was still on my bed. I hadn't touched it.

"STROMA!" I shouted at her, and she stopped dead on the bottom step, three paces from my room. "STOP MAKING IT SO HARD FOR ME TO LOOK AFTER YOU!"

"I'm not," she said, but she stayed where she was.

"Yes, you are. You're six and life's hard enough and you can't know everything so stop fucking trying."

"You sweared," she said, and her face started to crumple.

I thought, *That's right, but who have you got to tell?*

She sat down with her arms on her knees and her forehead on her arms. I went in and got the letter. I put it in my pocket next to hers and I took some deep breaths while she cried.

Harper called from downstairs, "Everything OK up there?"

Stroma shouted, "NO!" and I shouted, "YES!" at the same time. Then I sat on the landing floor and ducked down to look up at her face. There was a teardrop at the end of her nose.

"Look," she said. "I made a puddle of tears."

I thought about being Stroma, being sad enough to cry and then noticing the puddle on the floorboards and not being sad enough any more. I put my arm round her and I said I was sorry I shouted at her. I said it was for her own good.

"I hate secrets," she said.

I said that sometimes they were better than knowing.

"Is that why you won't let me tell Mum about Jack being Bee's boyfriend?"

"We can tell her," I said, "but not today. We have to pick the right day."

"And is there a right day for you to tell me your secrets?"

"Probably," I said. "Maybe. Yes."

The letters were burning a hole in my pocket. I wanted to read them and I was scared to read them and I didn't know what to do. I couldn't talk to Harper about them because nothing was getting past Stroma now she knew something was hidden, and I couldn't risk her finding out. The only way I could think to get away from her would be to lock myself in the loo. But then I'd be on my own, reading suicide notes from my mum, with nothing but loo roll and Domestos and old magazines for comfort. I'm not saying there's a perfect way to do something like that. I don't think there is. Just a better one, that's all.

Dad phoned to say that they'd moved Mum to a ward and she was asking for me and Stroma and we should come in. He said they'd had "a long talk". I wondered if Mum had done much of the speaking.

When we got to the hospital, Harper distracted Stroma with the vending machines while I slipped in to make Mum look better. Dad was in there, sitting by the bed, holding her hand. She let me brush her hair and we put a cardigan on over her gown so Stroma wouldn't see the bandages. She winced when we pulled the sleeves over her arms. She looked pretty awful still, but Stroma didn't seem to notice. She let go of my hand as soon as the door was open and she bent her head to Mum's chest and spread her arms over her.

She said, "Did you have a nasty fall?" Mum looked at Dad and he looked at me. "Are you all better?"

Mum just nodded and stroked her hair.

Stroma got something out of her coat pocket. "I made you a card. I didn't think I'd be able to because Mrs H doesn't even have one coloured pen, but Bee's got loads so I stayed up specially and I made it then."

It had a picture of Mum on it, except she was smiling, and it said GET WELL SOON at the top with about three hundred kisses. When Mum opened it, a clump of squashed flowers fell out on to the bed, moist and flat and browning at the edges.

Stroma said, "Why weren't we allowed in?"

"Where?" Dad said.

"Our house. Mrs Hardwick wouldn't let us in our house. Except Rowan did, but I didn't."

I kept my eyes on the wall.

After a pause, Dad said, "It was messy."

"Rowan told me. All splashed with water, but Harper cleaned it up."

"Harper?" Dad said, and Mum closed her eyes for a second, rolled them up in her head.

"*Rowan's boyfriend*," Stroma whispered to Mum behind her hand like they were two old ladies on a bench. "*He's lovely.*"

Harper was sitting in the corridor. He stood up when we came out of the room.

Dad was embarrassed, I could see that, and he wanted to say something. He was surprised and uncomfortable and exposed. Talk about dirty laundry.

I took Stroma to buy a hot chocolate. I didn't want her hearing anything she didn't need to hear. She was craning to listen even while we walked to the machines. The hot chocolate was too hot and too watery and too sweet. Stroma spilled some on her hand and it burned. We couldn't find anywhere to dump it so I had to drink it.

We watched from where we were standing. Harper was taller than Dad. He rubbed his hair with the palm of his hand, leaning into it, small circles. He put his hands in his pockets and twisted a little from side to side, his arms dead straight and tight against his body. Dad was doing most of the talking. Then he held out his hand to shake Harper's, and Harper said something and Dad smiled and gripped the side of his arm with his other hand, like he really meant that handshake, like it said something that maybe he hadn't.

Harper was smiling when he turned to us. He said, "Your dad thinks you should go home and get some rest, eat some food. I said I'd take you."

"We've just been home," I said. "What about him?"

"He wants to stay here." Harper shrugged. "He wants you to go."

"I'm not hungry and I'm not tired," Stroma said.

"God, I am," I said. "Come on, Stroma. Let's leave Mum and Dad on their own for once. You can have sweets."

"*Any* sweets?"

"Maybe."

"Orange Tic Tacs?"

"No way. You *know* you bounce off the walls when you have those. Anything but those."

Harper nudged her and winked and said to me, "You'll be asleep anyway. What do you care?"

I phoned Bee when we got out on to the street.

She said, "How are you?" before she even said hello.

"I'm OK. She's still here."

"Thank God."

"Step one anyway. Just because she didn't… you know, doesn't mean she's any better."

"Anything you need I'm here and so is Carl."

"Thanks, Bee. Thanks for Harper too. How did you do that?"

"Oh, he wasn't so hard to find."

"You've no idea how much better I felt just for seeing him."

"Of course I do," Bee said. "That's why I did it."

I went to bed in my mum's room. I didn't hear a thing – not Stroma (*Sing-along Songs* apparently), not the phone (Dad), not the door (Mrs Hardwick, "worried sick"). I was properly, properly out.

It was dark when I opened my eyes and the house was dead quiet.

Harper was reading in the sitting room. He looked up and smiled and put his book down and stretched. I watched him, with his perfect teeth and his dark eyes and his long body. I thought, *How did I end up with this beautiful boy on my sofa?*

"Hey," he said, and his voice turned into a yawn. I asked him where Stroma was. "Asleep."

"What's the time?"

He shrugged. "No idea. You want something? You hungry?"

"No, it's OK. I'm going to get a drink. Do you want one?"

"Why don't I get it?"

"Because I'm up," I said. "I'm awake now. Stay there."

It was one thirty-seven. I thought about where Dad was, if he'd had any sleep yet and if I should go back and see him.

"He called," Harper said. "They gave him a bed and he's staying the night and he'll see you tomorrow. Don't go there now."

"What did you two talk about before?" I asked him.

"He said thanks for cleaning the bathroom, kind of."

"What did you say?"

"That I didn't want you doing it. That it was easier for me. That he shouldn't sweat about it."

"Is that what you said?"

"Yeah."

"Does he know you're here tonight?"

"I told him I'd stay."

"And he was all right with that?"

"Sure he was."

"How'd you manage that?" I said.

"I told him I'd take care of you. I said I wanted to look after you because you've been looking after everyone else for too long."

He said it like it wasn't much. He said it like he'd overheard it on the bus or seen it on TV. He had his arm stretched out along the top of the sofa and his legs under the table. I drank my water while he was talking. I drank the whole glass and then I kissed him on the mouth.

He put his hands on my face while I kissed him, and then he smiled and said, "What was that for?"

"Don't be stupid," I told him.

We slept in our clothes with one of Mum's blankets on us. I didn't think I could sleep any more, but I did. I woke up early, watched the light grow around the edges of the curtains, watched him. I didn't want it to be tomorrow already.

"You OK?" he said before I knew he was awake.

I was thinking about the bathroom. I said I was afraid to go in there, even though I knew it was all gone. I said I wanted a shower. I said I felt like I did when I was nine and Jack told me there was a kidnapper in the attic. I used to run down the stairs too fast because I was sure there was someone behind me.

"Go on," he said. He stroked my arm with the back of his hand. "Get it over with. You'll feel better."

The bathroom looked completely normal. The sun came through the blind in stripes and things were back to their usual colour. The dust-coated rubber plant was unchanged by what it had seen, even if I wasn't. I pulled the curtain across the bath and I turned on the shower and my clothes made a pile on the floor. I washed my hair and I had the water a bit too hot. I stood with my face in the stream of it and Harper was right. I felt better.

When I picked up my clothes, I heard the crunch of

the letters in my pocket. I carried them downstairs with a towel around me and I sat on my bed. I looked at the handwriting on the envelopes. I knew what pen Mum had used. One of the fancy felt-tips that she'd bought Stroma a few weeks before Jack went on his trip. When Mum was still a mum. It was the darkest green one in the tin.

I couldn't open Stroma's letter. It was none of my business what Mum chose to say to her when she thought she would say nothing again. I didn't know if Mum was glad to not be dead. I didn't want to know.

And when I thought that, I knew I couldn't read my letter either. How can you read someone's dying words when they aren't dead but they wish they were, and nothing you can do will keep them alive and you're so angry with them you can't even feel it yet? It didn't make any sense. I couldn't say goodbye forever and then hello again.

I got dressed and I went downstairs and I gave them to Harper. I said, "Can you keep these, because I can't."

"Sure," he said.

"Somewhere Stroma won't find them. She really mustn't find them. I don't want to find them either."

"What are they?"

"More letters from dead people," I said.

twenty

I went to the hospital on my own. I walked to the bus stop. It was cold and the sky was clear and the moon was still out, faint and white, like a cut-out cloud. I wanted to get Dad a cup of coffee or something, but I only had enough money for the bus fare.

He was up when I got there. Up and very stale in his bloodstains and his nearly beard. Mum was still sleeping. I persuaded him to go home and have a shower. He didn't want to leave her; it was like he'd suddenly forgotten they'd been living apart for two years.

"She'll be fine," I said. "I'll sit with her. Go on."

He kissed me on the top of my head. "I won't be long."

I thought, *Does he reckon I can't manage without*

him? and then I remembered he might be right.

Mum was grey like someone had painted her skin. She had dark shadows round her eyes, but at least when she opened them she said, "Hello."

I asked her how she was feeling, but she didn't seem to know how to answer that. She wanted a sip of water.

She said, "Did you read the letter?"

"No," I said.

"Burn it," Mum said to me. "Don't read it. Burn it."

"Really? I can't…"

"Promise me," she said. "I don't want you to read it, Rowan."

I wanted to tell her she shouldn't have written it then. For a minute I wished I had read it. I was suddenly desperate to know what it said. It's like that thing when someone says to you, "Don't think of a red balloon," and there it is in your head, straightaway, bobbing up and down on the air, uninvited.

"I won't read it," I said, and I was wondering what the hell she might have put in it that was worse than what she'd done. "I hid Stroma's already."

She closed her eyes and sank a little into her bed. She looked exhausted, even though she'd just woken up. We sat there and it was quiet, except for the beeping of equipment and the voices in the hallway. Mum didn't speak so I didn't either. Sometimes she'd open her eyes and look at me and I'd smile. But she just closed them again, went back to the darkness behind them.

I was scared and lonely and bored. I wanted Dad to come. Or Stroma even. I wanted to see Harper. I made a list in my head of the reasons Mum decided to try and die.

Jack. Jack. Jack. Jack. Jack.

I could almost hate him for taking her with him when he went. But that was her fault mainly.

Me and Dad and Bee and Stroma, we missed him too. We wanted to turn time back and keep him with us. We longed to see him and hear his voice and enjoy the company of his moving, breathing body.

But we also decided to carry on living. And she was the one making it hard.

I wondered what would happen next, if Mum got better, if she ever got better, or if we'd be on suicide watch from now on. I didn't want to take it in turns to keep her away from scissors and ropes and light sockets. I didn't want to worry about her any more.

I watched a pulse ticking on the side of her head,

the veins blue on her arms, the set of her mouth.

I hardly knew her. Being alone with her was harder than being alone.

I sat there twiddling my thumbs and thinking about my brother. I tried to remember things I hadn't thought about in a while. Like the time we were watching *Escape from Alcatraz* and he said it was OK to look, so I turned back just in time to see Clint Eastwood lose his fingers with a meat cleaver.

Or the time he and his friend Ben hid under my bed, listening to me playing boyfriend and girlfriend with my dolls, until they couldn't keep their laughter in another second and ran pointing and spluttering from the room.

Or the day my hamster TinTin died and he helped me make a shoebox coffin and dig a grave. And how he didn't laugh even though rigor mortis had set in and TinTin looked pretty ridiculous.

I tried to imagine Jack aged twenty and thirty-five and sixty. I invented new memories. I wondered if Mum was lying there thinking about him too. If we had at least that much in common.

When the nurses came past to fiddle with her drip or

check her chart, they'd glance at me once and then pretend I wasn't there. Maybe they didn't know what to say to a kid whose mother just tried to top herself. Maybe they hadn't signed up for that training course. Maybe they were just way too busy to be nice.

For a minute I thought it might be me, turning see-through. It wasn't only Mum who hardly noticed me in the room.

But Dad could see me. He came in looking clean and shaved and still pretty sleepless. He picked up Mum's hand and kissed it, and she carried on pretending to be asleep. I could see her eyelids tremble and flicker with the effort of it.

"Everything OK?" he asked, crouching down by my chair, bouncing slightly on his ankles. He was trying so hard to be upbeat.

I shrugged and nodded and picked at a bit of fray on the side of my jeans.

"She been awake at all?"

"Sort of," I said, meaning, "She's awake right now, but she's trying to make us disappear."

"Has Dr Alvarez been?" I didn't know who that was. I said a nurse had been around, and someone else who maybe wasn't a nurse, but I wasn't sure. "What did they say?"

"Not a thing," I said.

I asked him how long Mum was going to be in the hospital. He said that was for Dr Alvarez to decide. "Another day or two, I'd have thought. They probably need the bed after that."

I thought about the queue of future emergencies lining up to take Mum's place. I thought about being in the house with her and her bandaged arms and her skin the colour of pulped newspaper. I started to feel shaky, not so you could see, just on the inside.

"What happens then?" I asked. "What are we supposed to do then?"

Dad put his hands on my knees. "Everything is going to be fine."

I hate it when people say that, people who have absolutely no idea of what's coming next. They turn you into an idiot for even asking.

"What evidence are you basing that on, Dad?" I said, and my voice came out too high-pitched and too fast.

"It's all right, Rowan."

"No, it's not. She's not ready," I said. "She's going to

go back to the house and sit in the dark and ignore us again and think about dying."

Mum shifted in her fake sleep, but she didn't argue. And nor did Dad straightaway because right then Harper held the door open for Stroma and she kind of burst in, mid-sentence. I could hear the orange Tic Tacs shaking around in one of her pockets, then the door closed again on Harper out in the hall. I could see the shadow of him through the glass.

At least Mum knew she couldn't go on being asleep with Stroma in the building. She opened her eyes and actually smiled. Stroma took this as an invitation to climb on the bed. She lay with her feet touching the bottom and her head on Mum's thighs.

I got up. I was going to leave the room for a minute and get some air. I felt like someone was stealing all my oxygen.

I was halfway to the door when Mum cleared her throat. She said, "I do want to get better." Her voice was small and cracked and fragile.

"Good girl," Stroma said, patting her on the arm. "Good girl."

* * *

Harper wasn't there any more and I went downstairs in the lift to find him. The doors were about to close when a family got in. Part of a family – a mum, slightly older than mine, and a boy about twenty-one and a girl maybe Jack's age. They were tear-streaked and swollen-eyed and still crying. The boy had sunglasses on and I couldn't see his eyes, just the tremble in his mouth and his tears falling. I knew that I was watching the saddest day of their life. I didn't even wonder about it, I knew without question. Someone they all loved had died. I was watching them and I couldn't stop and I knew I should look at something else like the floor or the walls, but I didn't.

And then something happened. As they walked into the lift, each of them in their own island of grief and loss, they smiled at me. The woman first, then the daughter, then the boy, smiling at me, some staring nobody in a lift, the same instant their hearts were actually breaking. I smiled back and I thought how incredible that was, that they would find the time to smile. There was goodness in the world still, even if you couldn't always see it. Maybe that's what Mum had forgotten, that even when you'd lost everything you thought there was to lose, somebody came along and gave you something for free.

* * *

In the end they let Mum out on the Saturday. I guess she promised them she'd behave, and they filled her up with happy pills and released her into the wild because they wanted the room.

We missed the homecoming. That was Dad's idea. He said it might be hard going. He said Mum might need some time. He said he'd stay.

It was such a luxury, having someone else do the thinking.

Harper took us to Bee and Carl's, about as far away from the planet my family were on as you could get. Carl opened the door. He picked Stroma up with one hand and shook Harper's hand with the other. Then he put his arm round me and kissed me on the side of the head.

Stroma jumped down and skipped off to find Bee and Sonny.

Carl said, "How's your mum? How are you, all right?"

"She's not great," I said. "She's home. My dad's there."

"And you?"

"I'm OK."

"Getting looked after?" he said, smiling at Harper again, shaking his hand again, patting him on the back.

"Yes."

"Good. About time."

"I just don't know what to do now," I said. "I don't know how long it's going to take or whatever."

"Maybe you don't get to know that for certain," Carl said. "You can't be in charge of what happens next."

"How's Bee?"

"She missed you. She's been worrying."

Sonny crashed into Harper's legs in the corridor and Harper picked him up. "Hey, little fella," he said, and they studied each other. Sonny was picking his nose.

Bee came in the kitchen then and smiled her beautiful smile and hugged me.

It was like a magic trick, to have a night like that on the edge of so much sadness.

We made a puppet theatre out of this enormous cardboard box Carl found by the bins. We painted it outside on the walkway and Carl cut a square hole for the stage. Harper undid one of the seams and stood it upright so you could hide inside it. Bee stapled red fabric to the outside for curtains. She had loads of hand puppets and finger puppets and string puppets. Stroma laid them in rows on the sitting room floor. She wanted to know all their names. Sonny kept walking off with them.

We drew a backdrop (trees, grass, a couple of castles) on a roll of lining paper and gaffer-taped it behind the stage.

The first show was supposed to be *Sleeping Beauty*, but it was more Stroma giggling inside a box than anything. Sonny was jumping up and down and the whole thing was shaking. Stroma's sleeping princess trembled violently and kept disappearing out of sight. She poked her own head out of the side now and then, to show us how funny she thought the whole thing was.

Then Carl and Harper did something about a woodcutter and a crocodile. Sonny clapped and squealed from start to finish. We could see the tops of their heads because they were too big to hide properly. Stroma said they looked like hills.

Later, Carl got Sonny and Stroma to help him make fruit salad. Stroma claimed to know all about it because she'd done it at school. "Except the knives weren't sharp enough to cut anything," she said, "only bananas. So

Mrs Hall did it all at break time and she chose me and Gabriel to help in the staffroom with the teachers."

"So I'll sit back and let you do all the work," Carl said.

Bee called after him, "Fingers!" and he put his head round the door and said, "Right you are."

It was the first time the three of us had been together properly – Harper, Bee and me. I couldn't help thinking it was Jack who pulled us all together, by doing nothing, by not being there.

I wondered if they would have been my friends if he was alive, or if they'd have only been his. If things hadn't changed, if Jack was still alive and Mum was like before and I was the old me, acting up and mouthing off and looking out for nobody, not even myself, I doubt they would have known me. I wouldn't have known me.

Bee would have nodded at me in the corridor because I was her boyfriend's little sister. Harper would have walked past me in the street maybe, that's all. We might have noticed each other and we might have not.

And here they were, feeling to me like they were pretty much all I had in the world. I told myself that some families we get without asking, while others we choose. And I chose those two.

I think that's what you'd call a silver lining.

"Some week," Harper said, and he put his arm round me and drew me towards him.

"Things get bad and then they get better, right?" said Bee. She was curled up in a big green armchair, her arms around her knees, her hair washed and combed and golden.

I nodded. "Just when you think they're never going to."

We were quiet for a bit then, comfortably quiet, all together. Sonny and Stroma were giggling furiously in the kitchen and the sound of them made us smile, like it was contagious.

"I was thinking of making something for your mum and dad," Bee said.

"What sort of something?"

"Well, for all of you really. Like a book. Some of my photos. Some pictures of Jack."

I thought about my Jack picture hiding under the bed, Bee's Jack picture, the picture that started it all. How greedy I was not to share it.

"Do you think it would be OK?" Bee said. "Do you think they'd want it?"

I said I thought it was a great idea. I said I could help. I said, "They should meet you anyway, when things calm down a bit. Or now even. I don't know."

Bee focused on me really hard for a second and then she looked up at the ceiling.

"You don't have to meet them," I said. "If it's a bad idea..."

"No, it's not that. I'm just— There's something else," she said. "I have to give them something else. I have to tell you something."

"What?"

"Is it private?" Harper said. "Should I go?"

Bee looked at me. "That's up to Rowan."

"God, no," I said, leaning into him. I was thinking, *What else could she possibly have up her sleeve? What else could she be hiding?*

"What is it, Bee?"

She shifted in her seat. She pulled something out from underneath her. More photos. She looked at them and then back at me.

"I don't know how to say it so I'm going to show you these." Her hands shook when she passed them to me.

Baby pictures. Newborn baby pictures. A baby

wrapped in a blanket so tight you could hardly see its face. A baby sleeping and wrinkled and impossibly small. And Bee, looking younger and wiped out and happy. Bee staring at the baby and smiling. Bee kissing its tiny hand. Bee sitting up in bed with the baby in her arms.

"Is that Sonny?" I said

"Yeah, it's him."

"I don't get it," I said, looking up at her, the idea closing in on me from behind.

"Sonny's not my brother, Rowan," Bee said. "He's my son."

The room seemed to shrink around me while I listened to her. I was staring at the pictures. Harper put his arms around my waist and held on.

"He's mine and Jack's."

twenty-one

When Jack died, Bee was two months pregnant. She didn't know it yet.

When he went away and never came back, he'd already left a part of himself behind. A cell constantly dividing, a mathematical miracle, a son.

She never went back to her old school. She'd had time off anyway, so she could stop crying. She didn't want people talking about her; she didn't want to be looked at or pitied or despised. The fifteen-year-old who should've known better and was messing up her life.

Bee said it didn't feel like that to her. She was scared and everything – scared to tell Carl and scared of being a mum and scared of what was happening to her body.

She said, "I always wondered what I would do if I got pregnant, like my mum did with me, way too young and all over the place. I wondered if I'd keep it. But when it was Jack's and Jack was gone, it felt like he hadn't left me with nothing. I felt like I wasn't alone."

Harper said, "It's amazing. I can't believe how amazing it is."

I was waiting for Sonny to come into the room. I was wondering which parts of him were my brother. I was watching the doorway and I was trying to take everything in and I could feel this thing, like a gathering snowball, in the centre of my body. Hope and excitement and an ending that wasn't final.

"Did Jack know?" I said.

Bee shook her head, studied her hands. "No, he didn't."

She said my name and I looked at her. She said, "I'm sorry."

"Don't be."

"I should have told you. Our families should have known together. If I could go back, things would be different."

"If we could do that, Jack would still be here."

"I know."

"You did OK, Bee," I said, and I was crying, but I wasn't sad. I hugged her. "You did more than OK."

Carl came in the room then with Sonny and sat him on Bee's lap. "Thanks, Dad," she said, and she smiled at him and he winked.

He put his hand on my shoulder. "You all right, Rowan? Are you taking all this in?"

I nodded and smiled and wiped my face on my sleeve. Sonny was drinking a bottle of milk. He played with his hair, his eyes slowly closing and then struggling to open, his lashes thick and dark like Jack's, his golden skin like Bee's. I reached out and stroked his soft and honeyed arm.

"Hey, Sonny," I said.

Stroma walked in then and stopped in the middle of the room like she'd forgotten something. "Why's everyone so quiet?" she said.

Everyone looked at me. "We're thinking," I said.

I was still stroking Sonny. He looked at me over his bottle and smiled. A little milk leaked out of the side of his mouth and trickled down his cheek towards his ear.

"Thinking about what?" Stroma asked. Then she saw the pictures in my lap and said, "Ooh, babies. Is this me?"

"No," Bee said. "It's Sonny."

"That's who we're thinking about," I said.

Stroma looked through the pictures. She said, "Why do very little babies look like old people?"

Carl laughed. "What do you mean?"

"All screwed up and grumpy and stuff."

Bee said it was because they'd just been woken up after a long sleep.

Stroma looked at her for a minute. Then she said, "Why is there a picture of you there instead of Sonny's mum?"

The room was so quiet I could hear the air bubbles pooping inside Sonny's bottle. Bee looked at me.

"Tell her," I said.

"Tell me what?"

"I am Sonny's mum," Bee said.

Stroma put her hand over her mouth and I could see all these thoughts making shadows in her eyes, like she was trying to add up too many numbers at once.

I held out my hand to Stroma and she took it and came to sit in my lap. She was thrown. She was trying to work things out.

"Do you want to know who Sonny's dad is?" Bee said.

"Is it a secret?"

"Yes."

"Then yes, I do."

Bee and I spoke at the same time. We said his name exactly together: "Jack."

I had no idea what Stroma was thinking. She put her thumb in her mouth and frowned at a place in the air just in front of her. I tried to look round at her face, but she just kept staring.

I put my mouth to her ear and I said, "Do you want to hear something funny?"

She nodded, but she didn't take her eyes off Bee and Sonny.

"You and me are aunts," I said. "You're Auntie Stroma."

She looked at me like I had no grasp on reality, like she had no idea where to start. "I can't be an auntie. I'm *six*."

Harper laughed and rested his head on my shoulder from behind. "And your mom and dad are a granny and a grandpa."

"Are you OK?" I asked her, rubbing her leg with my hand.

She looked at Carl. "If Jack was here, he'd be in big trouble."

"He'd be a dad," Carl said.

"That's weird," she said, wrinkling up her nose.

Sonny finished his milk and climbed backwards off Bee's chair. He started dancing to no music on the rug. "Am I still allowed to play with him?" Stroma asked, getting to her feet.

"Of course you are," Bee told her.

"More than ever," I said.

Later, Harper and I sat at the kitchen table with the lights off and the candles burning down. Everyone was asleep. Stroma and Sonny were sleeping with Bee in her bed. Harper held my hand, traced the lines in my palm. I couldn't switch my thoughts off. I was racing.

"When are you going to tell your folks?" he said.

"I'll tell my dad first," I said. "I'll tell my dad and then he can decide what to do next."

He smiled at me and said something like, "You mean you're not doing this alone?"

I pulled a face at him. "Do you think it will make them happy like it's made us?"

"I hope so."

"I want it to make everything better."

"Your mum's got nothing right now. Nothing that's working. This is like a gift."

"Do you think they'll see it that way?"

"I think Bee and your brother are about to change everything."

"I'm scared they won't," I said. "What if Mum and Dad are all judgemental and weird? What if they don't like her? Or don't believe her?"

"Don't be scared. Don't think like that. You worry too much."

I looked at him in the guttering light and smiled. "Where would I be without you?"

"You'd be fine."

"No, I wouldn't."

He stretched out his arms and yawned and got up off his chair. He started clearing the table. "Do you want to sleep in the ambulance with me?" he said. "We've never done that."

"Where shall we go?"

"Wherever you want."

"Let's go to 71 Market Road," I said.

"You serious?"

"Yep. I like that place a whole lot more than I used to."

We left a note. We said we'd be back first thing. We

parked up in the little turning where I'd seen him that day. We drew the curtains and made the bed. I found a book of pictures on a shelf, photos of Harper's family, of his mum and dad and of him, younger and smaller and just the same.

I sat under the blanket and looked at them. Harper was watching me. "What?" I said.

"I never expected you."

"What does that mean?"

"I picked something up and I gave it back, and that was supposed to be it. I was going to be in Madrid now, or Dublin. Somewhere."

"I'm sorry."

"No, don't be crazy. I met you and I didn't want to go. That's what I mean. I wasn't expecting that."

"Thanks," I said because it made me feel so good.

He laughed. "You're welcome."

I said, "I'm glad Bee dropped it and I'm glad you gave it to me. That one little picture changed everything."

I thought about Bee waiting all that time to tell me, not knowing how to do it. I thought how strange it was, looking back at it, how scared she'd been to share something good. I said, "Poor Bee. She must have been dying to tell someone."

Harper was still looking at me, but he was quiet for too long. "I still have to go, Rowan."

"Where?"

"Wherever I'm going."

"Are you leaving?"

"I wanted to see all these things and travel. It's my dream. I need to do it."

"Can't I come?"

"You know I'd love that, but you've got to stay here. You've got to stick around for this one, haven't you?"

I nodded. "And then what?"

"I need to go home and see my folks and tell my ma to stop worrying and – family, you know?"

"You're my family," I said. "It feels like you are."

"So I am. And I love you for saying it. And I'll come back."

"No, you won't," I said. I got this picture of him in my head, on the move, warm in the sun, everything new, the picture of me in his own head fading to nothing.

"Don't say that," he said. "That's not fair. I'm not lying to you."

I said, "When are you going?"

"In a week. Maybe two. I've got to make myself do it."

"I can't believe I'm not going to see you," I said.

"Look," he said, "I can't believe I met you, and you are so young and so much older than me, and I feel the way about you that I do. From the day you didn't want to take the negative out of my hands. You messed up my travel plans from the beginning."

"It's why you shouldn't go," I told him. "It's why I don't want you to."

He was quiet for a minute. He was thinking. "The way I see it, Rowan, we know something we're kind of young to know already," he said. "That's all. We've got more time to enjoy it. Does that make sense to you?"

"Jack and Bee didn't," I said.

"We're not Jack and Bee."

"I just want to be with you," I said. "I don't mean to make this harder."

"I have to go," he said. "For a while, a few months. I'll write. We'll talk on the phone. I'm not leaving you. I won't do that."

"OK," I said. "OK."

"I'm sorry, Rowan." He got up and he sat close to me on the bed. He put his arm round me and I leaned into him and I shut my eyes.

"I'm coming back," he said. "I promise you."

"You better."

I looked into the dark centre of his eyes and I thought about him being gone and how things might be when he got back.

I thought about Bee and me and no more secrets and how much I loved her.

I thought about Sonny, about what Bee and Jack had given to us without any of us knowing.

I thought about Mum and Dad.

I thought about Mum looking at us when we told her. I imagined her arms held out to Sonny, her hands on his skin. I thought about her telling herself Jack wasn't all gone, not quite.

I thought about her coming back, just a little, just in time.

I thought about us being a family again. Not just Mum and Dad and me and Stroma, but Bee and Sonny and Carl and Harper as well. I thought about us all together, at birthdays and picnics and long Sunday lunches.

I thought about Bee in Jack's room, touching each thing, feeling the trace of him on her hands. I thought about her sleeping in his bed and wearing his clothes and looking in his books for secret things he'd left behind.

I thought about taking it apart, the Jack Clark museum, and sharing his things because he didn't need them any more. I thought about having a proper room, breathing life into it, and nobody minding.

I thought about us going, all of us, our two joined families, to Jack's lake. Rowing to the island, soaking up the sun, burning our feet on the rocks, swimming in the water that took him. Seeing for ourselves what a beautiful place he left from, what a perfect day he'd been having.

I thought about seeing Harper again after not seeing him. About how that would be.

I looked at his face and I committed it to memory absolutely, and I said, "If I've done all right up to now, the next part is going to be easy."

Thank you thank you thank you to

Veronique Baxter
Laura West
Stella Paskins
Gillie Russell
Adam and Adele for
the Map of the Universe
and Alex

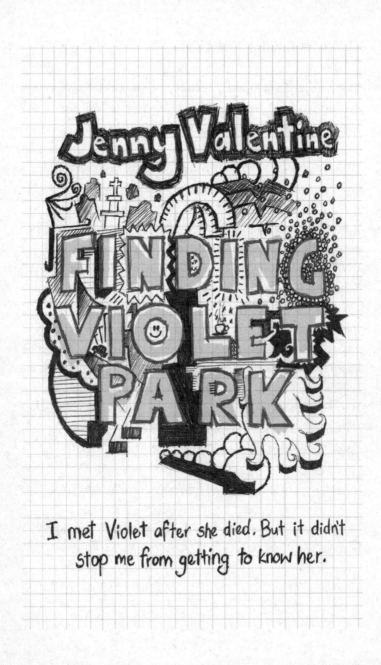

Jenny Valentine

FINDING VIOLET PARK

I met Violet after she died. But it didn't stop me from getting to know her.

Praise for Finding Violet Park

"A wonderful debut for many reasons… What marks this book out is not just its charm, warmth and wit, but also the skill with which Valentine braids together the threads." *Guardian*

"Ultra-original and brilliantly written, this will have you laughing – and crying too." *Mizz (Jan 07)*

"Clever and totally assured, it is hard to believe that this is a first novel… No plot summary can do justice to the particular flavour of this book, both witty and with moments of genuine sweetness… Excellent." *Books for Keeps*

"Jenny Valentine has an original and idiosyncratic voice that is full of understanding and humour … The dialogue is great, the observation is spot on. Valentine has a perfect sense of comic timing, [it] had me laughing out loud in some parts, made my heart ache in others … Has the originality of Mark Haddon, the immediacy of Jacqueline Wilson and the emotional connection of Kevin Brooks. It really does work." *Jill Murphy, The Book Bag*

"A great story, with a witty and believable main character." *tBk*

"A captivating novel from a compelling new voice in teen fiction … hilarious and dramatic in turns." *Liverpool Echo*

"Valentine captures the dynamics of contemporary family life without compromising the voice of her 16-year-old narrator… Amongst the drama, poignancy and desperation there is also optimism and humour." *Scotland on Sunday*

"Prepare to be thrilled and chilled … A challenging and disturbing read that lingers in the consciousness." *Schoolhouse*

"This is a terrific book." *Gateway*

Reader reviews

"I loved every page of this extraordinary book; a completely unique and involving story… a great book which deserves to be read over and over again." *Redhouse review, Hannah Pitts age 15*

"If Jenny Valentine doesn't start you reading, I'm not sure what will … A very creative and highly original plot … I would also recommend it to sneaky parents who like to snoop around their children's bookcases. But make sure you have time to spare, as you will be unable to put this book down!" *Emily Decker, South Wales Argus*

"An unpredictable story full of suspense … If you are looking for an original, creative, page-turner that is filled with mystery, look no further." *Megan Davies, South Wales Argus*

About the author

Jenny Valentine moved house every two years when she was growing up. She worked in a wholefood shop in Primrose Hill for fifteen years where she met many extraordinary people and sold more organic loaves than there are words in her first novel, *Finding Violet Park*. She has also worked as a teaching assistant and a jewellery maker. She studied English Literature at Goldsmiths College, which almost put her off reading but not quite.

Jenny is married to a singer/songwriter and has two children. *Finding Violet Park* won the Guardian Children's Fiction Prize in 2007. *Broken Soup* is her second novel.